HERE LIES DEIRDRE RACHEL EAMES

A Novella

Lazarian Wordsmith

Cú Mara Publishers Ireland

... sometime around the year 560, Saint Columba became
involved in a quarrel with Saint Finnian, over a psalter.

Columba copied the manuscript and intending to keep the
copy. Saint Finnian disputed his right to keep the copy.

Thus, this dispute was about the ownership of the copy.

King Diarmait mac Cerbaill gave the judgement,
to Finian, "To every cow belongs her calf,
therefore to every book belongs its copy."

Dedicated to the pals of my youth who shared the journey that began in our Midland Irish Town.

CONTENTS

INTRODUCTION

About Lazarian Wordsmith

In Ireland of the distant past, names denoted trades.

John Carpenter, David (the) Smith, Jack Miller, Billy Farmer. These are translations of the original Irish names. When I decided to use a pen name I followed the tradition. Since my third name is Lazarian and I wanted to write well, I aspired to be Lazarian Wordsmith.

Lazarian Wordsmith is an evolving human being: trying to live life to its full potential - among the Fingal Hills- in Ireland.

In another existence he has been an actor, broadcaster, script writer, historian, environmental campaigner, a radio producer and he also worked in the Airline Industry. His friends deny this - saying he was employed there.

He tries to craft stories on the anvil of his

imagination.

Sometimes he even succeeds....

HERE LIES

Deirdre Rachel Eames

A Novella

Lazarian Wordsmith

© 2022/2023

PROLOGUE

Anna Collins stood and waited while her Daideo Willie Collins, continued the ritual of breaking a pony. Well, he wasn't her real Daideo, her real Grandad. They just called him that. He was adopted, the story went, by the family a long while ago: and nobody knew the story after so many years had passed.

She watched while the animal trotted in circles, first one way then the other, while he halted, stood, and then ran and cantered and trotted again. All the time she strained her ears to hear the commands given or see the signals thrown from the hand down a long rein to the halter, but was unable to determine any instruction at all. In truth, in the brightness of the day she could not even see the rein. Yet there must be one: otherwise how could Daideo control the animal.

Yella Man Collins, was a small, hunched man, with an over big head, long out-sticking ears and a crop of wild red hair that at times stood high on his head, or lay matted tight after he took off his green bonnet. You could never call his headgear a hat, or a cap, only a long triangular bonnet. When he was in argumentative mood his beard and his ears bristled and moved with a motion known only to their owner.

Daideo Willie, liked people, onlookers, who came to watch him train ponies to be mesmerised at his skill, without rein, or whip, or spoken command to control the animal.

Anna knew that this illusion did not tell the story of the long hours under the full brilliance of a cloudless full mooned sky when those implements were used to train the animal to a stage where they were not required.

Fairy Magic Dust Willie called it. Anna's dad called it fairy cuteness.

Daideo, greeted her as usual, "Well Geartla. How's the care?"

Like always she replied, "I have no care."

Then he chuckled and finished the statement for her, "That's right, You lot, the family, are my care. Today's task, Anna, is for you to start writing down the story of my secrets. No! A Manuscript, Bedad! It will contain the secrets of the Rath Mór, the fairy home. I'm old now well over the allotted span."

"How old are you Daideo? No one can tell me."

"That's because I never told any of them. Let's say that the span of a man's life is long behind me, and the span of my fairy life is nearly over."

"I thought fairies were immortal?"

"That's what we tell the humans, but in my case living here, a changeling, among the humans has shortened my years. But that's old pishogues! I need to start the telling. Give you the tools, to carry on some of my magic. To give you some fairy gifts. To tell you all the secret cures to be found in the woodland and hedges, and the bogs. And also to learn you how to follow your dreams."

IN THE OLD TIMES

Late in the evenings after farm work, the men and women gathered inside by the fire to sing, play music, dance and tell tales of ghosts and of times when the fairies from the Rath stole the cat's milk or sometimes something more precious. Many a person told stories of people who, they said, had spent time away with the fairies. Really away: living with fairies, not just imagining that they did.

"I mind the time," Daideo Paddy told the people. "When them scamps above in the Rath, came and took first born sons away and left wizened auld men in the cots in their place. People dressed boys in petticoats to try and fool them. Long ago my family tried to burn the place down, but the fire kept quenching. So the people say they came and took the first-child and left a fairy in his place that grew up as one of the family. That's why some of us Graces still have a trace of yellow skin. The Yellow Graces they called us back then. We never knew where the gold was though. That's why we had to work to live. No harm in that children. Work never killed anyone yet: as far as I know, but you never know what some of those Cinnaths get up to with their excuses to be idle."

On harvest night just like most nights Paddy walked around his house and outbuildings checking on the animals. When he was satisfied all was in place he attended to his last chore of the day: carefully spreading his water with the wind while watching candles and oil lamps flutter and glow in the cottages along the road and across the railway track, where the tradesmen, ploughmen, horsemen and the labourers and their families lived.

Then he went indoors carefully ignoring the sounds and whispers of the young people, talking, giggling, telling their own stories of hope, and generally getting to know each other just as he and Mary had that first time they met at a threshing .

"He's gone in."

"I thought he saw us. Stop. You can't go there yet. It's not a safe time."

"Jakers, Molly, I'm like a rock. I can't walk home bandy-legged."

"Well look after yourself then."

"Will you not look after it for me."

"Scoundrel, you're named right."

"We will get married Joe won't we. They all say you're not the marrying kind."

"Of course we will. Easy, easy, take your time. That's too good a one to toss away quickly."

"Kiss me then Joe."

Soon they were courting as they say in the country, in the city they would most likely be regarded as spooning. After work was done most days, Molly would slip away to walk through the fields. He would be nearby watching to whistle guide her like a sheepdog handler, so that as she came through an entrance between the hedges that separated the fields, he had led her to his hiding place.

They talked about the future. Molly wanted to be married away from her family in a place of her own, planning to have a family. She craved money to be able to buy things: on the farm she worked for keep and clothes, but no money.

That the way it was then. If Molly wanted to leave home and work for her own keep she had little choices: a shop-girl, a domestic, a worker in the factory. That's what she had chosen when she abandoned her farm chores and went working in the sports factory. She worked stringing the tennis rackets, polishing the hockey sticks, packing the boxes and at breaks all the girls flirted with the boys. The most important lesson she learned there was the one that gave her the determination to be married and have a man she loved look after her. She flirted with the boys but a life as a factory worker's wife was not the one she planned for herself.

At the end of a year she returned to the farm still looking for a man but now her sights were on a businessman or a skilled tradesman, but mostly she hoped to marry a farmer's son, who one day would have the land.

But for the present, thinking like that was to be away with the fairies, dreaming of a place she could never reach. In the meantime Scoundrel was a diversion: besides her biggest fear was to be alone. Molly was never one of those people who were happy only to have an inner voice, to keep her company.

One night at a dance in a nearby village Scoundrel abandoned her once again: drinking with the boys he told her. Now it was different she watched him carefully and when he left the hall, as usual blending into the dark place along the hedges, she followed carefully: turning with the sheepdog whistles.

When she found them she stood motionless, hidden and listening. The talk was the same.

"Jakers Sally, I'm like a rock. I can't walk home like this."

When Molly got back to the hall, she found the older brother, John. Then she had her hysterical episode. She knew he would feel sorry for her and concerned that his brother had caused the distress. He took her home: cross-bared on his bicycle.

Ten months later just a month short of her twentieth birthday they were married. John was thirteen years older and had a very good job with the local Flour Milling Company: he was responsible for determining moisture content, before he mixed the grain, then ground the kernels to make the flour, that made the bread, that fed the town.

"Better to be an old-man's darling," she told her sister bridesmaids, "than a young man's slave."

The family housed them in a country cottage,

almost in the shadow, of the Rath, while he waited his turn to be housed by his company in their workers' accommodations. He had his eye on a two-up two-down town house where the current miller, who would soon be the master miller lived: with such a promotion came a move to a larger house.

He still went out early each morning to hunt, he saw this as a necessity if they wanted meat or fish: even though the war years were over, when the only place you could get meat or fish was direct from the land and the rivers.

Most days he brought back a few rabbits, and in season pheasants, partridge, trout and once or twice a salmon fresh from the sea running, up high, over stone, pebbles and gravel, into the mountain streams. Molly was content; what she was not spending on food she could squirrel away in her sock-drawer.

He made a garden and grew potatoes, cabbage, carrots, rhubarb, Molly loved making tarts. They fenced it in. The idea was that they would eat the produce and the rabbits: not the other way around.

When Molly told him she was pregnant, they cycled to town and later walked home: John singing and dancing along the moon-filled road, while she led two bicycles at her sides.

They still called him Old Bill: ironic after Young Bill was killed in the war. His wife Kate died that same year giving birth to what Bill called That Scoundrel. He cursed the Priests and their ilk. They said save the child, the new soul; you can't kill, let nature take it's course; the bloody medical man listened to them. He didn't understand: were they drunk, afraid? Of what? Hell's damnation. Didn't they know that for a man like Bill, left with a family and no woman that Hell was now, here in this life and anything that came after: salvation or damnation would be a relief. That should have been enough tragedy for one man to face in a lifetime. Now he had another crisis to face. Scoundrel had cleared off to England, with a local girl, he mesmerised into going with him.

At least he had The Weary Fellow fixed up. Maybe that was why Scoundrel did what he did, running away with the town girl to England. Bill always thought Molly and Scoundrel would be the pair. Molly was strong enough to break him from his wild ways: just like Bill had broken the spirit of many horses; made them come around to his way of doing things. On the rebound? Maybe that was why she married the older brother.

IN THE TIME OF JACK AND AOIFE

Jack Collins was asked to attend a fundraising function for the Irish American Society. Along with a group of workmates he decided to meet in a pub for drinks, before going. He was working and got delayed and then went straight to the function. It had not yet become a warm dancing, laughing affair, and he went to the bar and had a pint.

When his companions arrived, happy and laughing, a workmate Aoife, called him a louser, "I waited, watching the door, in the pub. You said you would join us. But that's you, always promising to join the party and then not turning up."

Jack was annoyed and as usual when in company with an attractive girl, he fancied, who he felt intimated him, was always afraid of appearing stupid in their company, so he retorted with a reply. "Look Aoife. I get paid to work with you lot. Not to socialise with you."

He saw the anger in her eyes, before he felt the slap. She turned, tears in her eyes, looking for the comfort of her friends.

Cowboy standing near enough to hear what had occurred, gave him the answer he already knew. "You're a Gobshite! That girl was waiting and watching the door in the pub: waiting for you. I tried to shift her and got the fish eye. Me The Cowboy, getting a rejection? Never happens! Don't be an eegit, follow her and say you're sorry. Whist! She's headed for the ladies now. Loiter nearby. But don't get arrested." Then he laughed and pushed Jack on his way.

A year later they married in Aoife's home place in Kildare. They made a home, and hoped to little-people it. In good times they hoped they would gather with her family for christenings, birthdays, communions and confirmations. They would join the other households in sickness and the sadness that marks the end of existing, of being, of life. Other times there would be loud-happy-laughing at weddings and those celebrations of the other days that peppered their lives. Jack was deeper in love that ever before, a love that had almost conquered all the memories.

Molly came to visit their new home, in the suburbs near the airport. She nosed into the rooms, even picking up opened, and still enveloped, letters from the mantle: intending to draw them out and read them until Aoife took them from her hands. She asked how much the house cost and how they got the money to buy it. Despite the look Jack saw on Aoife's face, clearly telling him to tell Molly to mind her own business, he told her they had a mortgage. A large mortgage, with monthly payments.

"So it's not really yours then!" She scoffed. "It's just like rent, you pay each month."

"Yes. Said Jack. "Just like you have the company house. You pay each week out of Dad's wages. But if we want to sell this tomorrow we can and pocket any surplus we get above what we owe."

"I never owed anyone, anything." Molly snapped.

It was not a good visit. Aoife told him not to leave her alone with her mother-in-law and Molly wouldn't go to the pub with Jack and John. He took them back for an early train: closing his ears to the comments on the life he had chosen.

"You have made your bed with that one, and you can live it now. I had a good girl in mind for you, from a good family"

Yes Jack thought and live down home, near you, available to drive you on Sunday Jaunts, and to visit your family. He almost laughed out loud, remembering all the rows she had instigated, with her sisters, on these visits.

John remained silent. Jack hoped he would speak with Molly later and make his views know: his views that would lead to a week of silence and sulking in the house on the street of The Brown Trout.

They were hoping to live that life, when a year into the planning, on a country walk, a youngster driving a tractor and a long trailer erratically tried to correct a swerve on the slimy clay, stones, and muck deposited by the back tractor wheels, over corrected and caught Aoife with the tailgate, left down and open, when it should have been upright and secure.

She was killed instantly. At the subsequent inquiry Jack learned that the driver was a child of sixteen with a driving licence to drive farm vehicles, in fields, not on a public road. The farm insurance did not cover such careless activity, and a judge later sentenced the boy to community care, explaining that it would be unfair to ruin the life of a young person with a custodial sentence.

Like a lot of other bereaved families living with the terror of a judge's social largesse for a killer: Jack hid his rage. Pushed it way down deep. Closeted with all the his other tragic nightmare memories, and tears.

Two women he loved lost to him, early in his life: and theirs.

IN THE NOW TIME

Auntie Anna was always telling them she was ready for her wings. When her husband Jim died and left her with a farm to run and a large family to feed: she told anyone who would listen that she would have her wings before this lot were off her hands.

When she had the kidney problems she was ready for her wings. She said it was not right for someone born in the early years of the Twentieth Century to live into the Twenty-first: surely she would get her wings before then.

All of her life was spent in a country place full of country ways and beliefs. She believed that hidden deep in her wood there was a magical, peaceful, timeless place, and that the hedgerow held cures for all illnesses: except old age. It was natural then that when the time came for her to really go and collect her wings; she would be true to her old beliefs. She took to her bed sent for Jack and told him her time was short: she had heard the Banshee's call.

"When she comes, I want you to answer the knock and sprinkle the salt and the earth: use her name, then ask her in. I've fixed up the lads with the farm and the girls get this house. I'm leaving you my wood, but you have to take The Lodge, and its tenant as well."

Anna stopped her flow of words, then tried to continued. She had something else to add and she was struggling. When she began again the words came quickly: she was eager to get this said and done. "There's one last thing. I should have told you long ago why Molly hated the little girl, for her own imagined fantasies, split you up. Well not the girl or you. The person she really hated was your Uncle Scoundrel, for dumping her and clearing off to England with her mother Hazel. In her delusions at times she imagined you and the girl could be related: that Scoundrel, your uncle was her father. The busybodies, in the town, said he and a girl ran away because the girl was pregnant. All Pishogues of course. Sometimes when her moods controlled her she was frightful. Manic depression they called those episodes in the old days, now they say Bipolar,. But your mother I would have said had neither she just had Jekyll and Hyde moods. Times when she knew she was completely wrong in what she believed, or imagined, but would never back down and admit she was wrong. At times she created a world where she believed her fantasies, and both of you suffered for that.

I should have told you earlier Jack, helped you make it all right, with the little girl. Helped both of you to have made it up. You should have visited when she was dying, Even after: there was a way. Yella Man's magical secret way, but I was scared you might change things. Change the past mess up your future."

Her strength and her time with them were going. "When they have my bones in the ground Jack - visit the little girl's grave. I'm sorry I let both of you down. There may be time yet to fix all that. Try hard Jack, make your dreams count. Go to the wood, dream Jack, dream there. Go inside the Yew tree. Ask The Yew Fairy and Astarte to help."

They sat with her. She waited, then near dawn roused herself. "She's here - outside - Jack." He opened the door and scattered the salt and the earth and invited the Banshee in.

"Aoibhinn. Beanshee to the Dal gCais families. Come in."

He moved back from the door to find he was shivering, cold, and very sad.

WHERE THERE'S A WILL THERE'S A WAY

"Well then, that   fixes it! We are in right shite here now!" Carmel was reading Anna's letter that instructed the family on her funeral arrangements.

"The Parish Priest will have a kitten. No bloody prayers, no flowers, no music, no speeches…"

"Good woman Anna," Jack chortled, until he saw the look on Carmel's face.

"Shit Jack, it's serious. Although I find the idea of an old fashioned funeral laughable as well. She always said she would do this. She had a thing about it, since the mother of the bishop got a send off with a crowd of priests and the like to sing her way into heaven, while Nan The Duck's coffin, she died around the same time, was stuck out of the way in the mortuary chapel. The Auld Dear said there was a priest for every week of the year up front wailing on the altar and Nan down in the back in the company of spiders and cobwebs."

Jack knew there was going to be a fight that Anna would have treasured.

The priest argued, pleaded, and tried to cajole. Finally Eamonn closed the discussion. He told the cleric in no uncertain terms what Anna wanted and why she wanted it that way and then delivered her final thoughts on the matter.

He took a page from his inside coat pocket, unfolded it, searched in a few pockets until he found his reading classes, perched them on his nose, and read.

If the clan of the round collar, don't, like the arrangements, or kick up a fuss, bury me in the big clearing in the middle of my wood. Let the Yew tree be my marker. If someone tries to stop that, just bring me out in the middle of the night, better still: near dawn, and burn me up.

And tell everyone I want my marker to read Anna Collins. I was a Collins before I became a Cody. Let it read as well. Devoted Wife to the late Jim Cody.

"So that's it Father, what's it to be? The graveyard of the funeral pyre? It's your call."

The priest stalled, left the meeting to ring the bishop. The family went for lunch and didn't return to the church. Late in the evening Eamonn rang the presbytery and was told that the bishop did not approve of the arrangements. However in the face of cremating a catholic woman in the full glare of the publicity he knew they would attract: reluctantly he gave permission to have Anna buried in sacred ground, the Parish Graveyard. But he thundered His

Grace insists on a proper funeral Mass. Eamonn sent his regards to the bishop and told Father Peter, to remind His Grace that the land for the new portion of the graveyard, and the new church was part of Fowler's Fields from the time when Punctilious was a Papyrus Skiff Pilot. He said to also tell the bishop, Anna would have often have told the family, they got it for free. They got it Buck Shee.

IN THE MOURNING TIME

The funeral was big. A woman who lived so long deserved respect. He stood with her family as people sympathised: each agreed it was time for her soul to rest.

He kept his back to the area of the graveyard where Deirdre lay. When he attended other burials he left by the small gate in the wall nearest the bridge, he never visited her. Now he turned to follow his shadow, a pathway guide painted by the climbing sun, to her.

She wasn't alone any more: her heart broken parents, were buried beside her. That in itself caused a pang of sadness, a slight tightening in the chest, a queasy feeling down low in the stomach: a memory of a time when he thought that in the end, they would lie side by side. It wasn't anything they talked about, or even planned, but down there in that country town husbands and wives usually ended up that way: twin plots one headstone; beloved wife devoted husband.

He ran their song through his head. It brought

him back to the tennis hops. She always saved that dance for him. No, matter who they were with, once the record began, they left and found each other.

A soft, "Hello."

"Hello yourself."

She settled within his arms and they slow danced: her chin on his shoulder, their eyes closed bodies moving slowly in unison; stepping to the slow beat one-two-one, one-two-one, one-two-one, alone in a crowd, lost in their world; the one that Buddy brought them to.

Sometimes we'll sigh,
 Sometimes we'll cry,
And we'll know why,
Just you and I,
Know true love ways...

The townspeople were leaving to go back to their own lives. Only a few remained, dotted around the plots, at the resting places of their loved ones. The local solicitor, while paying her respects, had asked him to call in when he had time.

"I know she left me the wood," he said. "And the lodge." She replied. "Call soon, Jack. Hanratty would love a chin-wag. Talk about the old days. The Gang and absent friends." She settled her handbag under her left arm and nodded towards the area of the graveyard where Deirdre was buried. Muttering, "Too young, and a family tragedy...." She left the rest unsaid, and Jack couldn't help her.

He sat in the park on a bench beside the river. His thoughts were back in the hospital room as his mother waited to die: they were waiting for her final breath. One by one she called her sons and daughter to her and gave them their instructions. Firstborn and last he stood waiting: she never beckoned, just turned her face to him in the end with eyes that held no love; even in that instant when she died; in the final moment, when perhaps, she looked back and weighed her own life.

Two swans moved warily downstream, circling every now and then, checking back to see if they were being followed. Beneath them the channel would be dark, coloured with the run-off from the field drains. It would be cold: a shock at first. Soon the water-weight in his clothes would drag him down: into the rocks, the gravel and the deep holes; where the pike who afterwards would razor-tooth his flesh hunted. He stood, then walked towards the water.

Soft words have been spoken,
So sweet and low,
But my mind is made up and I must go...

THE FRENCH WOMAN

Brigitte Vignoles grew up in a small town in Brittany in a climate of wind and rain. While other people remained inside in the frequent showers she would go out into sheltered places and watch the changing colours of the fields under heavy grey or dark clouds. Often later she would ask her Grandfather, the painter, how he would mix his colours to match what she had seen. No matter how patient he was or how hard she tried to describe them he was never able to reproduce what she thought she had observed. Finally one day Grand Papa gave her a canvas and a palette and colours and brushes and told her to try and paint these hidden skies for herself.

From the first time she viewed the Malton Prints of The Custom House designed by James Gandon, she had been intrigued by the idea that one of England's finest architects should prefer to design buildings in Ireland and scorn the challenges of designing buildings for the Russian Tsars.

The visit to the Custom House and the

King's Inns and the limited view she had of Abbeyville, did not explain why. Perhaps this last tour to Coolbanagher Church, with its elaborately baptismal font, and the nearby Dawson Court might.

The early morning train was almost empty: the views of the passing scenery grew green and lush; the small fields and roads were being clothed in their underwear of budding leaves; the small stations bright, tidy, small road-bridge-side gardens filling with colour; the air seemed to grow clearer, carrying her eye to the Slieve Bloom Mountains, a hazy distance destination pointer.

She had thoughts of home Maybe this trip was not the best idea, maybe she should go home, settle in and do what the family wanted her to do. She shook her shoulders and her head, her body almost shivering. All that: making bad decisions, being lonely, being afraid, feeling guilty and confused, all that she hoped was behind her.

A line of taxis and a horse-drawn carriage waited for trade in the station yard. Salesmen, intent on a quick promotion tour of the shops and businesses in the town hurried their way towards the cars. The drivers waited to open the backdoor, tip their caps and offer the greeting, "Nice to see you again Sir." They knew this hire would be a days work. Brigitte took the carriage her humour brightening on the slow one mile clip-clop yup-yup journey to the hotel.

As she dried her hair after a refreshing shower,

she decided that her adventure was surely only now starting.

At the door of the hotel, she stopped to admire the imposing Elms across the roadway: the wide semi circular, gravel covered approach was now shade less, bordered only by the stumps of it's long dead sentinels. To the left she moved slowly through the Main Street lit by a sun still so low in the spring sky that it was unable to penetrate down into the narrow, town-house honour guarded avenue. She moved towards the open Market Square still ablaze with the light. Entering into brightness she got her first view of the seventeenth century Saint Paul's Huguenot Church.

Entering the building Brigitte stood, listening to the stillness in solitude, almost feeling the sanctity, and the atmosphere that leaked from the old stone walls. She moved up the aisle and turned towards the marble inset plaques erected in memory of the pastors of the church and the patrons who helped build it and of those who had worshipped there.

Brigitte had spent a long time within the comforting walls of the church, reading the plaques enthralled that in this hideaway in the midlands she could absorb so much of what she was now starting to believe could be a part of her heritage. She would call France later and ask her father if any part of their family history mentioned Jean Vignoles, Pastor of the church from 1793 to 1817 or Charles who was pastor after him until 1841. She would also tell him that she had made one of those milestone decisions we all make only a few times in a lifetime, who we marry, where we live, what we do for a living. A sign, a notice, had caught her attention. Beside an alley to the park, beside a stone embedded in the arch above the alley, that read Thos Hill 1845, was a small narrow two-storied town house. An estate agent : a sign in the small window had an engraving of a Gate Lodge: an advertisement that said FOR RENT.

The auctioneer told her that before any agreement was reached she would have to bring her to visit the owner for interview. He made a phone call, on an ancient device, black and large, with the handset connected by a snarl-ball of twisted telephone wire. When he was finished and about to brief her on the instructions for the visit to view the lodge and be viewed herself, a mobile phone small and neat, began humming and dancing beside him on the desk, around it went like Ring-a-Rosie children, he ignored it. When he saw Brigitte watching he picked it up. "Only for emergency calls Dear, remember. I told you will only be used when I'm out of the office. Bye dear see you later. It was a birthday present," he added by way of an explanation, that made sense only to him. "Missus Collins-Cody, will see us at three. I'll collect you at the hotel."

A MARKET DAY
HANDSHAKE

Anna Collins was a big woman, tall and still straight, she wore her silver hair piled head-top above a back bun. She wore a black skirt, a black cardigan and a red silk scarf tucked above the top unfastened button. On her feet she wore a pair of rubber wellingtons. "Farm-shod." She explained when she saw Brigitte looking at her feet. "Farm-shod. A farmer must always be ready for muck.

She sat beside a large blue Wellstood Range, that burned the wood and made the flame, that sizzled the breakfasts, cooked the dinners, and made the cakes: heating the kitchen as well, and at times drying the work-clothes on the nearby wooden clothes horse.

She went with Dunne the Auctioneer and Brigitte to The Lodge and brought them around, then she took them to the wood and they walked a few steps inside. She signalled quiet: a finger on the lips and resting on her white-thorn stick she leaned her head: listening to the sounds, birds, mice and voles rustling the dry leaves and twigs, the trees creaking in the light breeze and songs other mortals weren't attuned to hear.

"Young woman. Do you understand English? Well the kind we speak here. In this place"

"Some of my ancestors moved here during the Huguenot Persecutions. Pierre La Combre. Yes. Missus Collins-Cody."

"Cody was my late husband's family. I was always Anna Collins from the time I was born, and I'm still Anna Collins. I won't even let them put a double barrelled name on my gravestone."

Brigitte began to apologise, but Anna was back in full flow again.

"Well, well. Begob! Lacomber! Lacomber: that's the way we say it here. Some of them are still around here. Do you know any of these trees?" Anna gestured towards a nearby copse.

"A few. The Beech. Elm. Silver Birch, there. Holly and Yew up the back."

"What colours can you see?

"Where?"

"Everywhere. Girl, everywhere. Look carefully now."

"Greens, more that one shade. Bright white, silver almost up towards the sky. Yellow and brown on the floor. Lots."

"Grey?"

"In the scales of some barks, behind the leaves of the birch, blue-, grey...."

"Scales: in the scales of the elm bark. Them's

good words."

Anna held out her hand, palm open. "It's been waiting a long time. I think it's ready for you. How long do you want it for?" She asked, then answered her own question. "I'll give you a lease for a year - less a day, of course. Some kind of legal bullshit!"

Brigitte reached forward to shake hands. Anna took her hand, holding it at the wrist in her own left hand, before it reached its target. She spit into her own right palm and then shook hands vigorously with Brigitte. "A bargain made!"

Brigitte hadn't planned to stay that long: but just at that moment it seemed right.

BOY MEETS GIRL

Now after almost four leases Anna who had become a friend as well as a landlord was gone, as she always said she would do: for her wings and Brigitte on the way back from the funeral sat in the Town Park, on one of the many path-side benches.

She was eavesdropping: on the sounds of the river, the noises in the gardens at the back of the Town Houses and the calls of small children running themselves down into tired, refreshing, dreamy, all nigh-time sleep.

Two swans moved downriver. The man sat nearby, unmoving, reflective: he had salt and pepper hair, white to the front, speckled dark at the back. She recalled a pictured of a white pony running wild in the wind: mane flopping up and down, right then back to the centre again.. He was familiar: she realised he had been with the family at the graveyard.

Leaning back she raised her face to the sky, looking upwards towards the now amber-edged soft clouds. High, so high, that at first she could not properly identify it, the bird circled slowly, uplifted by the hot air rising from the cooler earth; it was outlined against the white of the clouds, then became obscured against the blue, then appeared again. Wings outstretched, catching the rays of the sun, reflecting them burnished, polished like worked copper. Its head wore a similar crown of gleaming light. Faintly she heard a cry... Meow... Meow a kitten sound.

Jack could see the light flash and glint on the water and the swirls of the current passing over hidden pools. No river sound reached him, only his voice mouthing the words that stuttered within him. " But my mind is made up and I must go..."

Now he was closer the flow of the current, clattering, singing, sighing and moaning overcame the singsong mantra, bursting so loudly into the awareness of his death, that it startled him and he halted. Another song reached him. He heard the call in the sky and knew it was a Buzzard. He looked up and saw the female. The sun glinted on her pale under wing feathers and he knew she was a young bird perhaps in her second year. He looked higher and saw the male begin to drop on his plunge of courtship.

Brigitte watched the bird as it seemed to stop in mid-air. Another bird plunged downwards as the first flipped sideways and stretched its wings outwards. Protect yourself! The attacking bird stopped its downward plunge and stood air bound briefly, wings beating, standing as if to offer an embrace. Then together both birds swooped in unison, down, then wings beating strongly, together up, then wings outstretched, swooping, down again. The smaller bird broke off and started to climb alone, rapidly with strong quick wing beats, higher, higher almost too high to follow. The larger bird circled slowly below. The small bird is going to attack again, she thought.

She stood and moved off the path and onto the grass. Jack walked backwards eyes still skyward. They converged.

She adjusted her balance and turned searching for the climbing bird. Jack was close enough to get the first faint waft of her perfume. He lowered his eyes and looked at her. She had short dark hair, high cheekbones, a wide mouth and full lips. His gaze was drawn down to the upturned neck. Her skin was tanned like polished mahogany yet alive, pulsating, and strangely inviting.

Sensing his presence, strangely unafraid and comfortable, without lowering her head she asked "Aigle? An Eagle?"

"No!" He answered softly as if the birds might hear him and stop their display. "Better! Once they were endangered: now they are making a comeback - Buteo buteo - Buzzard Hawks; very old species, native birds, magical birds."

"A fight? She asked. "An onslaught? One will kill the other?"

"No! Boy meets girl. A mating dance, courtship"

She could hear his breath whisper the words as

if they were holy words, sacred words; lowering her eyes for the first time she looked closely at him.

He was engaged with the birds, his blue eyes flashed.

"Look! He's climbing for another pass. She will circle and wait. When he is close she will flip and dive with him. We might have a result - a pairing here.

The bigger bird was circling lazily, unhurried, checking, waiting. The cock bird located the female then folded his wings, streamlined his body feathers, lowered his head and began another dive.

Jack turned to keep the birds in view. Brigitte turned quickly; the heel of her shoe caught the kerb: she staggered and they collided. He reached out and held her. He noticed the gold cross around her neck and the division of her breasts below. His hand brushed along the outside swell of her right breast. The sensation of a breast resting naked in his hand with the nipple hardening in the heel of his palm filled his thoughts. She turned, swinging her arms and her body for balance. Her hip came into contact with his lower body; she saw his eyes flash blue again.

Above, the birds screeched together in a final plummeting dive. Still looking skywards they parted: then together said "Sorry."

'I'm Brigitte."

"I'm Jack" he replied.

"I saw you at the funeral. They told me you are my new landlord?"

"I am. It seems."

They walked, talking, blubbering in the novelty of each other, side-by-side, across the park. If anyone had asked they would have been unable to explain why two people who had just met could be comfortable in each others company. For a while the pain inside him went away.

Later she tried sketching the birds and the mating ritual, each time the drawing was of a smiling mouth, blue eyes with desire in them, and a silver-mane As she put a third drawing into her bundle of sketching, she was happy that he had asked, and she had agreed to let him drive her to The Lodge, even if he didn't come in with her.

MADIGAN'S HARBOUR BAR

Jack drove away, not on any planned journey automatically he changed the gears, negotiated the twisty roadway bends, going nowhere: but recognising his destination when his automatic pilot took him there.

Old Bill's favourite oasis on trips in the days of the Bona Fide, that law that required Sunday drinkers to travel three miles before they could visit a pub. It had been an inn, on a large harbour at the end of the Grand Canal branch that was constructed to carry barges of coal from Castlecomer to Dublin, but had not been extended any farther. The pub looked as unfriendly as ever, slates had updated the thatch, a new set of double-glazed plastic feather edged windows had replaced the tiny square paned ones, the faded sign still proclaiming Madigan's Harbour Bar.

Inside, the cobble floor displayed the stains and grime, that no amount of scrubbing could remove. The tables were converted sewing machine stands, the large foot pedals now used as footrests.

Above on the smoke stained wooden ceiling relics of the canal age hung on pegs or were attached to the rafters: wheel spokes, items of horse harness, caps, bells, buckets with faded barge names; even large thigh waders and fishing rods and reels. Jack knew that if he searched around he would even find a stuffed fish in a glass display cabinet.

He ordered a Jameson and ice and sat inside the patio doors to the harbour.

Jack finished his drink in one motion of hand to glass, glass to lips, liquid to mouth and heat to belly. Beyond the harbour the light cast shadows away down the towpath. There in the past among the horse hoof prints, and the call of boat bells, ghost called to him. He left Madigan's Harbour Bar: this time he knew his destination.

THE LODGE

The wood had changed: not just in the growth of briars, ferns, and the offspring tree shoots reaching for sustaining light; it was different in brightness and sound. The paths that he once knew so well were hard to find, the places they went to were hidden again, the pines no longer whispered - here. In here. Their haven was lost hidden again in the bramble festooned shrubbery.

Somewhere near, he knew, lay the path they followed arm-in-arm inside the camouflage of the boundary trees, deep into their own secret place. There tree-nestled and tree-backed, she pulled him to her tiny slim body, to kiss her cool soft lips, brushing his cheek with her nose in a face beneath the short bouncy fair hair that painted a soft shadow above and around closed brown eyes: when open they were always smiling full of life and full of curiosity. She offered him her small breasts: released from her Mother's prison of a stitched-shut-bra. Her nipples hardening, seasoning against his chest as they stood ankle deep in the autumn-wood mulch; wrapped beneath his overcoat in the autumn winds that withered the leaves and carried them to the forest floor. They were conjoined trees: swaying gently, lip locked, beneath the moon and stars; spied on by pine martins, squirrels, owls and sleepy, hot-foot-hopping pigeons, on their battlement branch-perches of beech, oak, ash, elm and pines.

He walked around the outside trail all the way in a circle, back to where he started from. Just like the hungry grass that the old people spoke of. *At night, don't walk the fields. You'll get into a field of hungry grass and loose your way and keep going in circles.*

A light through the trees: the brightness of the whitewashed lodge gable, teased him out. Anna's Lodge: his now. The lodge she refused to live in when first married content instead to live in the Collins family home. All attempts to get her to move was met with the simple answer, "It's not ready for people yet." Jim offered to modernise it. "Doing it up won't make it ready for people," she insisted.

Over the years she watched the weeds and wild grasses and the blackthorns surround it and then years later when Jim was dead and she was alone in the home farm with her own family around her: she began to get the lodge cleaned up. They conquered the briars, cleaned the paths, got the farm workers to paint inside and whitewash outside. Tradesmen were hired. The kitchen was updated, a new bathroom and shower installed, the chimney was cleaned, a solid fuel stove drove the new heating.

She offered it for rent. Families came and soon went again: the remoteness and the proximity of the trees on stormy nights, offered as excuses. Then one day the Frenchwoman came looking. They talked and Anna offered her a lease. Brigitte moved in and was happy and stayed and Anna smiled.

Jack moved from the wood, sad again feeling alone: abandoning his hope of recapturing the feelings he had shared with Deirdre there. He moved around the house; the path away from the wood waited there.

Brigitte came out the door. Startled she stood back inside.. He turned to assure her, "I'm sorry for..."

She smiled, "Jack." Then following his gaze past her to the painting in the hall smiled again and asked "Do you like it?"

He didn't hear her. This painting couldn't exist: it could not be. Two young people had been captured in a dance embrace. The boy back to the viewer. The girl's face, chin resting on his shoulder. The short bouncy fair hair, a soft shadow above and around her closed eyes: brown eyes, that he had seen open, smiling, full of life and full of curiosity.

"Ho..how? Where? How did you..."

Startled by him, by his colour, and the sadness in his plea, she quickly answered, as if her answer could change him; pacify him.

"I was sketching in the wood. In my mind I saw them like this. I think perhaps they were lovers."

Softly he added, "For a while, for a short while."

JIVING AT
THE HOP

They sat in her kitchen at the back of the studio, the in-blown air carrying the smells of the garden. Jack sat sipping a second Brandy, the first had water-fallen quickly: burning then warming, then soothing. He sat, the painting on a table, propped upward by a Westminster Chime clock that ticked the seconds and chimed the quarters and bonged the hours: sharing with a stranger the story he had to tell; a story that in some strange way she had become part of.

He couldn't remember how they met. They drifted into being part of the same loose collection of teenage companions, who went to movies, to tennis hops, for countryside walks, for swims in the river and then later they went to real dances, dinner dances and functions, always a pair expected to be together.

Many times he tried to recall the first time he became aware of Deirdre Rachel Eames. Late at night unable to sleep, he tried to roll back the pattern of scenes, searching, examining, discarding, all the time hoping, to remember that first time: when his heart leaped and his insides churned and he felt weak with happiness. He was certain that was the way it had been: perhaps at the tennis pavilion on the Station Road, or the Hall on Foxcroft Street, across from her Grandmother's house.

They would have danced together: a jive? She liked jiving, her skirt swirling outward, body leaning backwards, for moments trusting his arm, his hand, his fingertips, to balance her and keep her upright, twirling and smiling, happy and laughing; and then just before she overbalanced to draw her back, upright and into his safe embrace.

They started to meet secretly at the pictures: her mother didn't want her around boys until she was older. She would sneak in just when the film started; wait while her eyes adjusted to the flickering twilight reflection from the screen, then vision restored she would find him. They sat together arm in arm snug and silent and watched the world of gangsters, cowboys and romance flicker its way into their young lives.

His story telling was slow, sometimes long pauses held the story traffic-jam bound while he waited to sort the images and find the train of events. On a long pause: one that breathed sighs that might end the telling, Brigitte entered the studio and brought back a small under-elbow of brown backed frames.

"Anna told me I would get inspiration in her

wood, I have more. People have been telling me their story for a long time."

"No." Jack said. "She has been telling you our story."

Brigitte went to change the picture but waited while the clock chimes played their zither salute.

WALKING
THE LINE

In the wood when the curfew time approached the companions signal-whistled their locations and readiness to leave; they all walked home, shuffling, laughing, kicking arms-in-arms in an overflowing avenue of hard crackling, moonlight glinting, leaves; some still drifting down confetti slow, joining their companion clutter on the narrow wood side country roads

He studied the painting: the Moon a waning crescent. A group of shadowy people, walking single file arm balanced, along the shiny beamed rails of the railway: they were skirting the town, above the houses and the distant bogs, where distant lights of late turf gathering machines winkled, criss-crossing the bog cotton fields, tilly-scrimping the final harvest. Above them stars: The Plough, Cassiopeia, Orion, Pegasus.

He remembered they even found the Galaxy in Andromeda: one dark winter night, young teenage eyes looked overhead at the two million light-years old candle-glimmer, that is the sideways Nebula.

On colder nights too cold for walks: they huddled together strung along the back row of The Picture House, paired again locked together, whispering, questioning, silently lip-reading the nods, and then content again, in their own snug place among a paper chain of low crouched silhouettes.

STILL WATERS

Brigitte offered another scene. "The Lock." He remembered the Canal and the Lock, the Barge and Branigan.

He left his street from her side street Deirdre would join him. They followed the long straight pathway and left the rows of town cottages to a place of solitary farmhouses. From behind they heard the clip clop of a horse approaching. A low flat hay cart drew alongside. His Uncle Chuck beckoned and they joined three children who sat, legs dangling over the back of the cart between the road and the see-sawing bogie. Through a gate they looked into a farmyard where a woman dressed in a long black dress washed clothes in a small bath, scrubbing the soaped clothes along the sideways leaning washboard.

Near the bridge that climbed up the steep and narrow bridge over the canal, they jumped off and waving thanks moved to the centre stone and looked beneath to the lock and the tall black water-keeper gates with sluices that leaked bright, splashing streams to the level below, and above in the higher stairs, to the harbour beside the grain stores, the swans, the water hens and the beds of green lilly pads with white lilly flowers.

A long, black, narrow barge puttered from the narrow upstream channel into the harbour, and waited for the lock side keeper. Branigan appeared in the splendour of his uniform: a black-grey suit, preceded by his fob and chain secured waistcoat and puffing pipe, beneath a thick grey moustache and a battered narrow brimmed hat. He went quickly to winch the splashing, noisy, water into the lower trough, raise the level then open the gates to capture the barge; then lowering the water to the lower level and releasing the barge into the lower stairwell of the canal, so that it could continue its journey.

Job completed the keeper returned to his green gated, rose-arched, cottage pathway, and stopped to remove his hat and mop his brow, checked his timepiece before entering the twilight interior to await another puttering summons.

They ran up the hill to the higher level and walked canal-side, past the hazel groves the hawthorns, greengage trees and the damsons, towards the castle and their secret place above the straight keep wall: conquered just like the high orchard barrier with pointed stanchions fashioned from the rusty hay turner.

High above the ruins, the dungeons and the lower staircases, moat-circled from invasion by the sedentary blue-green Grand Canal waters, and the diamond glitter on the tumbling darting, skirting Barrow river flow, on their regal seat in the window, beside the battlement walk, they kissed, hugged, sighed, talked and dreamed.

"And you painted all of these from visions in the wood? I can almost smell the splashing water and feel the spray droplets from the sluices in that one." Behind the painting he heard the unmistakable sound of the clock bell-spring winding its way to chime. The Westminster Chimes played the hourly salute, of o'clocks in the afternoon.

"Yes. I would walk in the wood and be inspired to paint. The scenes crashed onto me and then almost like I was a machine I painted these." Brigitte halted the exhibition. He was tired now. More mental than physical.

"I think we should halt, now. She offered. "Tea another drink? A rest?"

"Tea please. Yes. A break will help."

DARK STORM CLOUDS

He saw the next frame - a storm: a terrible storm. The colours: the blacks and the greys, the redish-yellow of the lightning forks; the fury, large trees bending under a terrible wind, leaves scattering, flaking, dying, torn apart while airborne. The dark clouds: pillows for the out of focus face and flying hair above. Her shoulders: the storm had to be a woman; supporting the mollusc arms with branch scattering fingers, long and taloned reached out. Searching for her victim.

Molly missed him again: knew he had skipped away. The spade handle in the orchard stood like a naked broken scarecrow. He was away with the girl. She gathered the baby and tossed her into the pram. Furiously she pushed out into the roadside path: this time when she found them she would end this once and for all. The bloody tramp would get him into trouble and then take him away from the town to Dublin or worse still to England. "I have plans for that Bucko, my girl", she muttered as she turned to where she knew they would be. "He owes me. He owes me a lot."

They were content, weary, low sugared from the day, arm-in-arm, slowly backtracking to the town when Jack felt wrath. Sometimes that happened: his mother would broadcast her fury like radar, searching for him, sweeping, probing, somehow locking into his consciousness. This time she must have been more agitated that ever before, he could feel her: then a vision: he could see her; on the straight road leading to the bridge, beside the sand quarry now coming out of that birth canal of tree branches over the road, pushing his infant sister in a pram.

He told himself he was having a daytime nightmare: she could not be there. When they came off the canal bank and onto the bridge she was waiting for them.

"Caught you. I knew where you had got to. I told both of you I don't want you together. No buts. No buts. You clear off Missy. You get home before me now."

Deirdre knew it was best to be silent. This woman before her on the road had lost her reason. What ever they had been doing did not deserve this: an innocent walk in the fields, and back home along the canal bank.

She walked away as the loud angry words began again.

"She's a tramp. I told you to keep away from her. Her family have a history, with me. You owe it to me. I gave you life. I gave you a home."

"I didn't ask to be born." Jack countered.

"I wish you hadn't been." She shouted.

As usual he muttered, I hope you enjoyed the sex at least. This time she heard him.

"Bastard. Don't bother coming home."

"I won't"

"See who else will have you. Just see."

Eventually, late in the evening, when he was sure she would have calmed down, he went home. His father was waiting, sitting alone before the turf fire.

"What happened between you, this time?"

"I was walking along the Canal with Deirdre. She came looking for me."

"A bad row?"

"Yes."

"I kept some dinner for you."

"I couldn't eat it."

"I know how you feel. She's gone again. Off on her bike to Josie's. She'll come back as usual in her own good time. I suppose."

Jack replied. "Some times I wish she would stay away. Then I could have a life."

John was not the kind of man who reacted or got angry quickly, or one who held things in his heart and let them fester into hate. He could see that Jack had a good point, but he wanted a quiet life so didn't tell him he had felt that way himself often in the past.

Molly went to her sister and walked the farm land, and went into the high fields, where the breeze cooled her murderous thoughts and took them away. When she returned home she told Jack he was going to live with his Aunt Josie for the summer months.

That was the Summer when his Godmother, taught him how to smoke, how to dance a waltz. In the evenings she took out of the cupboard the wind-up gramophone and records. To the 'Rose of Arranmore' she taught him how to waltz the old-time waltz: One-Two-Three, One-Two-Three, One-Two-Three. Swing.

The most important lesson he learned when Josie pointed out that a lot of girls came visiting. "See the young ones, they don't come here to see me. Work it out handsome."

Margo was older quieter: she had discovered literature and their walks were conversational, their resting places in the meadows two separate body forms: tidy and passionless.

Jenny was nice, with an outgoing personality, she kissed full mouthed, her tongue cheek squashing her bubble-gum. He went through the field-hedges with her and her brothers to set wire snares for rabbits. With the dogs they walked through the meadows flushing skylarks, pheasants and partridge and mocked the hare who ran wild and weaving before the dogs only to return again to her start point. They dug footholds in the quarry and climbed into the higher fields and into the double-ditches scattering foxes and avoiding badgers: wiry coated tanks who stood and fought instead of running.

At summer's end he returned home, a little older, much wiser and more determined than ever to defy Molly and keep seeing Deirdre.

A SMUDGY
WINDOW PANE

"What is that one there, the sketch at the back? Is it one of them? It looks different. Black and white, smudgy. Is it smudgy?"

Brigitte reached over and took up the paper. A charcoal drawing of a girl. A sad girl, standing inside a window, a sash paned two part, draw up to open the window. The figure was not clear, almost a shadow, but the hands, joined in a praying gesture, were well defined. The vista she was viewing was reflected in the glass panes. It was clearer and Jack thought he recognised some of the buildings, and behind that the landscape.

"Like the others, I got this after a walk among the trees. I don't know what it is, or if I will ever finish it. I think some buildings are a city: London perhaps. The fields I don't know where they are. Unclear not defined at all. Mostly just scratches, and shading."

Jack thought he knew the image, because in some way it reflected a scene he had participated in.

Deirdre went to London. She came home for holidays and festivals. He travelled down they met and talked. Once they even walked the mile to the wood, but it was summer, the enchantment was gone: from the wood and from them. When they still talked about the sky and the stars, some small magic remained: one night they got drunk together and agreed that on nights when the starlight was at its brightest; he would look out his window on Calderwood, and when the wind was blowing South he would whisper her name; she facing North from her window in London would listen for him faintly calling.

He made a life, in his work, among his books and in an occasional short relationship. He went on discounted flights: journeys to the sun, recharging batteries. He visited other continents and cast her name wind borne from beaches, gorges, hills and plateau. He cast his message to the Prevailing Winds, the Trade Winds and even from the Doldrums. As time passed he didn't whisper her name as often.

Finally one day in the plains outside Nairobi, newly married, with Aoife, looking north across the waving grasses that hid the lions that stalked the antelope, he stood content, silent and happy.

DARK PRAIRIES

One Christmas he was down home and saw Deirdre. She was hurrying: pub crawling with companions she brought home from London for the season. They looked cold natured, individualistic, uncaring. They kept moving, skulking away from even the dim street light, back into the tavern glare; to pull her once a creature of the brown black midland bogs, dark prairies under the night sky, back with them into the glare of the bright illumination squeezed by turbines from its heart-turf.

He saw her, eyes dancing jiving now in infatuation with a new adventure that took not only the life she had to live, but in the end her laughter and her strength.

On that night on the pathway they fought. They shouted out of control in violent anger in the storm of the battle; she shouted harder, moved her body in jerks, her arms trying to rise up to hit him but falling down before the blow. Her sister calmed them and told him to come and visit in London. She would get her alone. They could talk: maybe you can still talk to her; maybe she will listen to you: maybe she needs the cure of the home-town memories.

THE DOG BOX

The painting, was untitled. Just a wooden dog box, a kennel: empty, no happy faced dog, with a lolling tongue smile, and the suggestion of a wagging tail in the semi-darkness of the interior.

"You hardly got this idea from dreams in the wood, it has nothing to do with the story."

"Anna asked me to paint it for you Jack. She laughed a lot when I finished it. That's the ticket she said, give it to him when the time comes. You will know when to show it to him. And he will know what it means."

Jack was puzzled he didn't know what it meant or what significance, if any, this could have to the story of himself and Deirdre that Brigitte had been getting in "suggestions" from her walks in the wood.

"Brigitte, can I borrow it for while?"

"It's yours Jack. She told me it was for you."

"Hey girls, come and have a look at this. Jack has no idea what it means." Tess Conlon laughed, when Jack now back at Anna's house, put the painting in its frame propped on the kitchen table leaning against the wall.

She continued to laugh. Her sisters glad of an

excuse to break off on the cleaning up, after the wake and funeral, joined them and laughed loudly as well.

"The bloomin' dog house Carmel said."

"Ah! Shit. You should have made him guess what it was. It's the dog house Jack, surely you remember."

"No Janie, not a clue. Anna asked Brigitte..."

"Your tenant. Landlord." Carmel prompted.

"Brigitte," Jack continued to explain, Anna asked her to paint this, she told her what she wanted, and said to give it to me. An empty dog house, what's that got to do with anything?"

"Someone make a pot of tea, maybe lace it with something stronger, this could take a while."

The girls taking turns and sometimes laughing in amusement told him the story.

VINEGAR WITH EVERYTHING

Anna did not like lies, telling lies she said was part of a failure to communicate and the lier lacked courage. When it came to Molly on a rampage, in a black mood, searching for Jack when he went missing, she made an exception. But still she would not tell a bare-faced lie, she found other ways of protecting him. Molly would arrive across the gravel outside the kitchen door, throw the bicycle down and storm in. Before she could talk Anna would remark. "He's in the dog house again."

"He's run away again, the shagger, I was just talking to him and he cleared off."

"Talking to him? Or shouting at him?"

"He's gone. Did you see him?"

"No not a sign. What girl are you trying to stop him from seeing now?"

Molly's eyes would widen at the question and her face get redder, but she stopped at picking a fight with Anna. She always needed to get on with her story, tell her side before she calmed down. Her story in this state would be full of exaggerations and suspicions and very little facts, except those "facts" she believed, which were only imagined by her.

"That Walsh floozie. Her uncle sells fish. He's a road side trader. Her father runs the chip shop in Ferbane. She's over here on a holiday and they have linked up." I'm going to put a stop to their gallop."

"I though Johnnie was doing well, and had a restaurant now, not a chip shop." Anna carefully replied. It would be important to distract Molly, get her back on an even keel. She knew the breaking a plate over someone's head would not be far below the surface. She had been there when Molly and her brother in-law were washing dishes, and Din was arguing with Molly over a trivial issue.

"If you don't stop annoying me, I'll break this plate over your head."

"Go ahead," he said, lowering his head towards her.

And she did. She broke the plate over his head, and split his scalp, and then pushed the table and spilled the basin and all the rest of the dishes onto the stone floor and ran out of the house and into the fields.

So when Molly was in a fury looking for Jack she knew he would be hiding where she had advised him to go to: the unused groom's, room above the stables, still fitted out with a bed and other furniture. She called it The Dog House and suspected that Jack was there now. In all the years Molly never found him and Anna never visited him: that way she never saw him, or knew for sure where he was hiding.

"The dog house Jack, that's what she is saying to you. remember the refuge."

"Another bloody conundrum, that's what it is." Jack offered. "Another puzzle to work out. What the blazes has this picture to do with anything?"

Eamonn had entered while the story was being told. "I remember , once being sent out to see if you were in the groom's room, It was a long time before she told me it was the Dog House as well. But the question now Jack is, what clue is the old dear giving you with the painting. A conundrum indeed."

"Worse than you think. That reminds me. Do any of you know anything about someone named Astarte, or The Yew Fairy?"

The family began laughing again. "The old dear has this fella believing more of her tall tales. They are just characters she made up in the kid's tales she used tell us. Not real at all Jack, pure imagination. The Great Astarte the patron of resilience and success. I asked her to help me pass my exams."

"Did you Tess?"

"I did in me arse"

"Did you tell Anna?"

"I did and all she told me that Astarte had always been bull headed." Then she laughed. And repeated bull headed. You know the way she repeated things. The pot calling the kettle black."

THE KERNEL OF
THE PROBLEM

Hazel and Ben Eames had reared their family so that one day they would become their own people. Whenever one of the boys decided to leave home she supported them. Men could always look after themselves and overcome the obstacles that life placed in their way. Her girls would marry, probably around the district, and make their own homes and in time families. Deirdre had been raised just like the others, but she grew in mid-teens to be rebellious believing she was ready for her first step into relationships with boys. The Collins boy was nice, polite, doing well at his studies, and would have a good future. In time he would be a good catch for someone; maybe even Deirdre if she wanted to make a life with him. God help anyone though who had Molly as a Mother-in-Law: that woman had never been able to get on with her own life, without sticking her nose into other peoples' business.

Molly hated her, she knew that, ever since Joe, took her away to England and left Molly fuming. It was a wild wonderful romance. She was young in a big city. When Joe stayed away in the ale-houses, she went to the pictures and an occasional theatre show.

Eventually like all his girlfriends before her, Hazel was abandoned. Scoundrel, as his family called him, did a midnight flit.

In later years Molly insisted that Deirdre was Joe's daughter. She said it often enough to Ben. I know Hazel got pregnant when she was with Joe. That's why he dumped her. The fact that it was not true could never appease her. I know you are hiding things, she often snarled.

Her convent education, though sparse, compared to other girls from money, who could stay an extra year or so at school did in their exams, but Hazel's was just as good, since she was a good listener and would study hard.

An education is not a heavy thing to carry her father told her. Better for a man than a hod full of bricks. For a girl better than an early marriage and a bath full of dirty clothes: or worse still, kids on a Saturday night being bathed in a tin bath, before the fire.

So she thrived in various jobs: shop assistant, factory girl, barmaid, and finally as a ledger keeper in factory, hidden in the back office recording orders and deliveries, and as time passed balancing the money. She was able to earn a comfortable living and save a little.

Then Ben Eames came into her life, she fell in love. They married and had a baby girl. Homesick for Ireland both of them saved and dreamed and eventually Hazel brought Ben, and her daughter Deirdre, back to her home place, in the Irish Midlands.

Ben set up a small building company, and employed men, Hazel managed the office, did the orders, wrote the estimates for customers, balanced the books paid the wages: and the taxes.

ABOVE THE
RIP TIDE

Now if Hazel said her teenage daughter could not see the Collins boy, Deirdre would obey reluctantly just for a while. It would be better if they continued to see each other, let them get it out of their system.

They hid away passing each other on the streets as strangers. They changed to new secret places, out along the narrow gauge railways where the small steam trains and bogies carried the turf from the brown bogs to the Power Station. There in the wet-day shelters, alone now in the sunshine, they talked and laughed and made plans.

Did they make love? That's what they were at all that time: making love, more suited to their teenage years, above the rip-tide of the bikini line: before - before what? Television, promiscuity, birth control devices, the Cosmopolitan search for the ultimate orgasm - maybe all of those, maybe none of them

Their autumn foot-kicking in the mulch beneath the trees in the wood and their summer in their meadows full of hay stack high jumps and their springtime bog treks continued. If Molly's radar detected them she never came looking.

KEEP IT TO
YOURSELF

Molly was in her early forties when her local doctor sent her to Dublin, to Holles Street, for a scan. She was complaining of pains and other things that John said was women's complaints. It was then that they first discovered the tumours.

The uppity specialists asked Jack. "What do you do. I want to see if you will understand this."

"I'm a Computer Specialists - in The Airline." Jack answered. "What is there to understand?"

"Well," he continued. "You have an education so. We have to tell some family member what's going on and since you're here in Dublin you seem to be the one. Missus Collins," He went on, skilfully avoiding the emotive words - Your Mother. "Has a very virulent cancer. It's in her ovaries. She has about three months left."

He went cold. The voice inside him screamed. Manage the information. Manage like you are trained to do. Get this out of the way: panic later. He took a deep breath. "Have you told her?"

"Not yet. Today. We will tell her today."

"Don't tell her, nor my father: if he knows she will coax it out of him. She won't cope, won't survive the news, and he won't either. You hear me, I will handle it. I, will handle it."

Jack insisted that they move her to a hospital in Rathgar for treatment. She went through Radium Treatment. She was to some extent content because the hospital was Saint Anne's not Lukes: Lukes was reviled in the country as the cancer hospital; the last chance saloon, once they got you in there and opened you up - let the air at it - you were a goner; the oxygen made it grow. Never let them open you up!

He stood there beside the bed and lied evening, after evening. They haven't mentioned exactly what it is. They told me but I didn't understand the big words these shaggers use. Beneath his clothes he secreted his apron of protective lead while destruction pulsed inside her womb: trying to shrink the tumours.. The nurses warned the rays could make him sterile if he stayed too long. When he tried to leave Molly asked stay a little longer. The nights and days are long lying here.

His dad, didn't want to know about the illness, just wanted her back home, hale and hearty, cured. His God, the one he prayed to every day, the one he trusted, would make it all better. It seemed that his prayers were answered. She went home and her days of recovery outnumbered the frequent trips back to hospital for treatment.

Then one night she took a turn and was

whipped away to the local hospital. They were all called in. Files were consulted. Phone calls to the Dublin hospitals were made.

"Next of kin?"

" Talk to me." Jack said.

He was warned: this was it: she would not last the night. The matron met John on the stairs as he went up to visit his wife. She started to commiserate to say sorry we did all we could, but saw Jack slowly shake his head. Dad was confused in a situation he didn't understand and at that time didn't want to understand: the summons he didn't want to hear. If it's not said it may not happen. Jack got away with it. Afterwards the Matron asked and he answered.

"I never told him this day might come, this soon."

Later that night, Jack snoozed in a chair waiting: then their minds were joined again. They walked across the white meadow to the wooden gate, where voices clamoured inside the walled garden, the voices of people attending death's party that night. They stood and waited while she considered opening the gate. Instead they turned and walked back through the meadow to the gasping and awakening room together.

Over the months, that grew to good years and bad years The Cure, or remission, whatever it was, enabled her to put on weight, rejoin her family life, rear her younger children, watch them through their school and twenty firsts. She attended two weddings, and four christenings. She was a glamorous granny: on the outside at least. Inside, although the cancer was asleep or withering away - it must have been since it never got to kill her - other changes were happening. She became more domineering, tried harder to control her family, make them live lives she thought they should live.

Then Jack introduced his future wife to her, when she saw the ring, she burst out crying. Not in happiness but in frustration: the nice girl, from the nice family who owned the hardware shops, that match she had chosen was now out of the picture. She didn't give up. Comments about a second marriage, being a second-hand husband, getting used goods were common. She hadn't been listening when they told her the wedding ring Aoife wore had been her granny's: perched on the wrong finger awaiting the move to the ring finger. Molly knew they were lying to her. She knew, they were lying.

When they gave her the wedding date, she still didn't stop snarling, saying out loud that if it was too soon, and asking if a pregnancy was the reason. She hated couples who had to get married, she talked about early morning church side-door marriages, she talked about lives ruined, about dirt sticking forever, about people always remembering.

But she never mentioned her family secret, the one Jack found out about many years later after she died. Her mother had been one of those women she despised, and she had a half-brother, conceived and born outside of marriage. And he had an uncle he never knew, but had on several occasions passed him on the streets of their town.

Visiting the graveyard one day he met a cousin who enlightened him. *In that grave behind your Granny, do you remember Paddy Short Leg? He's buried there. Your Granny had him before she married your Grandad. He was,* and here, he lowered his voice, *homosexual.*

Now she turned on her husband, the quiet man, who loved her and the family without conditions. She forgot that he nursed her, when the pain and discomfort was intolerable for him because he could not lessen or remove it. When he could only offer ice cream for a blistered mouth, cool ice filled towels for the sweats and teeth clenching hugs in the owl-hunting hours of the long nights. At the morning when she slept weary and exhausted, he left the sick bed, left her reluctantly to the care of others, and went to work.

She ran away: he cared for the family. She came back: he picked up the broken crockery. She railed against neighbours.

Shopkeepers rob people all week and then eat the altar rails on Sunday. Farmers charge too much for milk and vegetables. Priests go to functions, drink brandy, dance with women, then say mass the following morning. Guards won't raid pubs, and run Sunday drinkers home for dinner, their poor wives have to get it ready, and then throw it out.

She picked on her own family sisters and brothers and when they called ran them from the house. The husband was blamed in the town when he turned visitors away: reasoning that it was better than rows.

Jack was asked to speak to her: they went for a walk; he said that for her, life, living, family, the seasons, the wind, the rain, should be more precious, considering her death threat so long ago.

Although he didn't tell her she had escaped cancer, because now he realised she knew – always knew it was cancer, but hid it away, never spoke about it but always knew she had it. He was now reminding her, of the real enemy she had hidden away and managed to ignore.

She said that knowing that would kill her, then she ran home, closed the door against him, and even in death never allowed her family to open it again.

When the scar tissue clogged her guts they operated to clear it. Later she sat up in bed and belched, smiled, laughed and talked with her husband. The next morning when they stood her out of bed, to ensure her blood would circulate, she had a fatal heart attack. When she lay waiting for her final breath she called her younger children to her and gave them their final instructions. Jack watched them: bedside crouchers, nodding and agreeing with what their instructions were. But he knew from experience the admonishment would be to never darken his door again.

First born but now last, he stood waiting. She never called, just turned her Janus face to Jack in the end with eyes that held no forgiveness; in the instant when she died, in the final moment when she looked back and weighed her own life, her spirit showed him why she always hated him.

It started on the day she discovered she was pregnant, being married, it was her duty to her husband to provide an heir, but in her mind at twenty years of age, she had some flitting around still in mind. A child, so soon, put a premature end to her plans to be an old-man's darling, rather than a young man's slave. Even if that young man was new born.

HEDGEROW
HONEYSUCKLE

The days of sun and nights of stars continued, the weeks became seasons, the seasons grew to years and then his father rang.

"Deirdre's back home - She's dying, some terrible wasting disease. Are you coming down to visit her? They don't want visitors but maybe they'll let you in."

He went on breathless, eager to explain. He had practised this, said it aloud to himself, listening to the words he already knew: to refine the inflection.

"Her sister brings her for a drive, that's where I found her sitting in the car near the wood. It's all changed. People walk there now on Sundays.

"She's going blind now too.

"What kind of sickness takes your faculties like that?

"She asked for you.

"Her sister said she sometimes cries in her sleep and mentions the old times. I think she wants to make peace between the two of you. You better come down while there's still time."

What would he have said if he went down, what would he have brought with him - flowers? No! Flowers die. It called for a more permanent gesture. The only other thing he would have brought was a memory: of a time when they were young; when all the summers seemed hot and bright and full of river-swimming; the winters were love-nights under the stars.

He stayed away, even though on still nights when the city traffic had dimmed and the windfall leaves rustled only quietly beneath the branches, when the scent in the air was hedgerow honeysuckle, he heard her calling on the soft, cheek brushing, wind, softly, softly, so faint, away in the distance. But he tried to busy himself with distractions, even attending functions and work gatherings that he had avoided up to that time.

His father, self appointed intermediary, continue to supply the news and niggle at his conscience.

THE GROOM'S QUARTERS

Jack remembered when the barn held work horses, used in the fields, and around the area delivering or collecting loads. Later it housed ponies trained to pull traps or other carriages.

Once the local undertaker housed his hearse there. An unfortunate accident with some bereavement candles caused his own storage yard to burn down. The hearse and the horses were out on an overnight job, and were spared destruction. While repairs to the buildings were ongoing, the business moved into what was now Anna's Haggard.

The groom's quarters were snugly constructed on the second floor over the stables. In one side wall a doorway gave access to a balcony walkway above the main area. Under the living quarters spacious stall housed the population of work horses, ponies and lighter carriage, pulling and prancing, horses. The heat from the animals, in winter provided an early and primitive under floor heating.

Inside there was a small kitchen and bedroom complete with two bunk beds. Originally grooms, stable-boys, or other tack room staff would occupy the premises when foals were expected or other horses, or ponies, requiring veterinary care, on a twenty four hour basis.

In Jacks time, hiding there, the animals had been replaced with farm machinery. The accommodation was still liveable and it was this room that Anna Christened The Dog House.

It still smelled the same, horses, liniment, for horse strains and human limbering up, harness oil. Not damp, or musty though. The girls, some of them at least had been doing a bit of maintenance, cleaning and polishing.

Jack lay on the lower bunk, on a slim mattress with squeaky springs. Why anyone would banish a good swingy spring bed for an interior stuffed mattress, with solid springs and a thick blanket, for a duvet, and a rigid base, he never understood that modification.

I used hide comics and those books that were banned in Ireland, up there under the boards above. The upper bunk had been made with a wooden platform, for a groom with what he called a bad back: a slipped disk. He got relief from sleeping on a hard surface.

No one, I bet has been in that bed above for a very long time, Jack thought. Wonder is it still firm. Maybe if I climb up there I will find out: then again maybe it will collapse and I'll fall through.

He climbed out of the lower bed and stood examining the upper platform. It looked intact, if he noticed it looked a bit hilly and uneven in the top corner. In a place he surmised where a reader might put a book, under a pillow. He stood on tip-toe and felt underneath. There was a book there. It was a small diary, held intact with two rubber bands. Various leaves of paper had been inserted between the bound pages. Jees, he thought, this looks like Anna's farm work journal. She kept the records of crop and tillage, and animal sales, and purchases in it. But when he undid the rubber bands, they disintegrated as he pulled them, requiring a quickness of hands and a change of his position to maintain the shape of book and inserts: he discovered it was not a record book.

This needs to be spirited out of here. It was hidden for a reason, and it was also hidden where very few might look for it.

SPELLING

"Well it's still there: The Doghouse, but someone has been keeping it neat and tidy, dusted, and polished."

"The old dear, had one of us look in now and then to make sure it did not get damp, or rundown looking. She told us she was keeping it for when you might need it again. She said the day would come when that fella' will come to his senses. Haven't a clue what she meant by that," Eamonn said.

Jack looked around the kitchen, where the girls were tidying and sweeping after the lunch. "Travelling over here is fine, but there are times when the hours that involves, could be spent better. Does anyone mind if I temporary move into the Dog House?"

Carmel smiled. "So you won't be shacking up with your tenant, then?

Ignoring her, but smiling Jack replied. "So it's OK?

"By the way. Anyone know what this is?" He queried taking the book, he had found out of his pocket.

"Probably her Spell Book," Tess suggested. "But I think that is her Cure Journal. She made remedies from plants and the like. For strange ailments. She said she had a bottle to cure most ailments."

"I remember her making a cure for Dad for some blood ailment or other. It worked and I asked him what was in it. And he said slugs and snails. A Maneroch bottle, anyone ever heard of it?"

Eamonn reached out to take the book from Jack. "It may be her Cure Journal, but it's not the one I remember. It's bulkier, more pages."

"Loose pages inserted between the bound leaves. I almost dropped them when I took it out from under the covers, in the groo...in the Dog House."

The girls were over the shoulder gazing, wondering what it was as well. Tess vocalised their thoughts. "It looks like her journal, but it's not. Neither is her cure book. The loose pages? Give us a look at one. Yes. It's not even her writing, she was a Copperplate Hand woman. These look like they were torn out of some kind of copy book: like a child's homework book."

"Spot on Tess. She would have called that a scribble, a spider's hand. Anyway I have a house to look after. Is it that time? And as the old dear would have said. Not a child in the house washed. I'm off. Give a hug to your lodger for me Jack."

"F-off Carmel. Slán. Come on Gang, make some tea. Let's sit at the table and have a goo at this yoke."

Several cups of tea, and a good amount of Sweet-cake later the book was assembled into bound pages and loose sheaf's in small piles on the tabletop. Some of the loose pages were numbered and that caused problems, several page ones, twos, and the rest made it difficult to know where to start their examination.

"Some of them have holes punched at the top or side, other look like they were stapled, or held together with a wire clip. More of the Old Dear's security plan."

An hour later Tess, Eamonn, Janey and Jack had what they thought must have been the original sequence. It hadn't been easy and they had to resort to trying to match half sentences with their companion words on the next page.

"Did ya get anywhere Carmel shouted as she came back in the door. The dog is fed and Foster as well. I couldn't wait 'til tomorrow, to see the results."

They separated the piles into manageable lots and started to try and read the sentences, random words, and in some cases doodles. None of it made sense.

"What or who was an Apothecary?"

"What was gallaces?"

"What was a rack?"

Suddenly Jack jumped up from table. "A rack for your hair. The language that confused the foreigner. It's Fingalian or something like it. The first outside settlers to the east coast arrived at the mouth of the Broadmeadow Estuary, the locals called their encampment Fingal, the land of the foreigner. After a while locals started speaking in their own made up language, based on Middle

Era English, which came in with the Normans, to confused the invaders. Tess do you remember Anna looking for the rack to comb her hair, or Francie looking for his gallaces, to hold up his trousers, and annoying Mam, by using common language. I came across it in Swords. How does it go now? Yes! Lawneydey it is Fingalian? I'm a Cinnit, for not seeing it sooner. Anyone interested in having a Barney with me for being so stupid? Now it's coming back to me Yola spoken on the south east coast as well as Fingalian, in Dublin, mostly the same words."

Carmel had been looking at the pages as Jack was speaking. "Hey lads this squiggle to me looks like the Auld Dear's Hand, writin' that is, before she went Copperplate. Like she was in a dream, or under the influence, while writing this."

Janie added "She was not a drinker, so she was not under the influence of drink, and she would never have done modern day drugs. Maybe just and old fashioned remedy for a cold or flu. That would be all she would take."

"Some of it looks like English, but if you study it, words with quare spellin', like someone was writing them phonically. Is that it Jack? Spelling them how they sound."

"Maybe that's it. I'm away girls to consult an expert on all things Fingalian. Off to Swords so. Gather up the pages and I'll be back as soon as I can."

"Slán, Jack drive safely."

As Jack was leaving Anna's kitchen table, Carmel said. "Will ya bring the lodger with you? A test drive maybe? Ya know run her in..."

Various voices replied. "F-Off Carmel."

Eamonn had been checking messages on his phone, as the rest were discussing the pages. He asked. "Surely in this day of technology you could scan the pages and e-mail them."

"Considered that Eamonn, but maybe these coded instructions, I think that's what they are, could be how to build a bomb, after all Cody was once one of the boys. Didn't himself and the Lea Man blow up the Police Barracks in Patrick Street. I don't want any copies of these around until they're translated."

AMONG THE FINGAL HILLS

Back home in North County, Jack rang his old friend Connie, together many years ago they helped to set up a local historical society. She was interested in recording the stories of her home place, and Jack was a blow-in trying to learn about his adopted home. Early on he suggested maybe they would write a book together. Now many years later Jack was book-less, and Connie was now on her twenty fifth offering.

She recorded stories from residents and produced them as Tales without Cats, local people telling of their experiences of growing up, their interaction with their parents, and other interesting happenings around the place. One happening was of a local man, Paddy Cleary, who travelled to Paris to get an injection of newly discovered Penicillin from Louis Pasteur.

As instructed on the phone call, Jack called into the Heritage Centre, in the old Carnegie Library in the town.

"Jack. I knew you would be back when you

needed help, with something or other." Connie had a sharp tongue, but she didn't mean to be nasty. The attitude was common among the natives.

Jack replied, "As usual, I see you are delighted to see me. What has it been now since the first committee meeting up the main street? Years? No decades."

"Well Jack both of us are still here and that's a blessing. Can I help you with something?"

"Can you speak or read Fingalian? They used speak it here."

"No I can't. No one can any more. But I have a few books here with partial dictionaries."

"Fair Fingal? Archer's book?"

"That would be one of them. Do you still drink tae? Or are you a Cappuccino man, now?"

"Tae, please. Connie. Can ya have a gaw at something for me?"

Connie looked at the pages, drank her tae, brewed some more. Then started on the first page, first sentence again. This time she mouthed the words in whispers. Jack remained silent, knowing that to interrupt her would get him a rebuke.

"It's not all Fingalian, some is the local English as she is spoke out here. See this first page, I think this is a help. It seems to be the authors name. 'Yellamon Buke'. Any clues what it means?"

Jack laughed out loud. Then recovered, "Richard was our Reader at Mass. God rest him. He would get up to read from the Book of Samuel. But he said, A readn from the Buke of Saml, in his North County Accent – a Fingal accent. This is a book of Yella Man's stories. I think he dictated this to a very young Auntie Anna, and she wrote the words as he said them. She believed he was a Fairy Changeling. Translating this will be fun."

"It's not all written in local dialect Jack, some of it I believe is real Fingalian speak. Good luck getting to the bottom of that. Do ya want more tae?"

"Connie I have to get back down to Auntie Anna's place. Thanks for all the help."

"Glad you came up for this goster Jack. Don't be a Gowerairah from now on."

"I won't be a Jack snipe. My path is true and straight, from now on."

Connie laughed. "It's coming back to you, but I was thinking of the other phrase for the Snipe, a goat of the air. As the youngsters say. Keep me in the loop. Want to know if you solve this conundrum. Slán Jack."

Before he set out to return to the midlands, he went home, and collected some dusty folders, stored away at a time when his heart was broken. The history research was something himself and Aoife did, travelling as a pair and visiting museums and archives together. In these somewhere was a Glossary of the Fingalian Dialect. The word for darling jumped out to Jack from off the first page, 'Ahaygar'. It also could be translated as beloved one.

MIDLAND TAE

As he had done many times, Jack sneaked back into The Dog House. The trip to his own house in North County and the memories stirred by retrieving the glossary, meant he was not, as yet, prepared to meet the family. Raw nerves of memory, and loss had stirred.

On the table were coffee, tea bags and a kettle, electric thank God, and still fresh milk. Over a steaming mug of tea, he started to compare the loose, but now sorted and assembled, pages with the glossary. Immediately he noticed not all of the words were clear and easily translated. Taking 'Brave' as an example he realised it was not meant as having courage, but in the way of the Cavan people: it meant a Brave Day, a good day with a Brave bit of sunshine, a Brave field of spuds.

Jack Críonna, old wise pal, rest in peace. When we drank together, you said we were not drinking, we were just Buddhelin, and there it was in the list: Ducks sipping for food in shallow water. We are only sippers of whiskey he meant, I see that now.

Next morning he joined Anna's family for breakfast. "Didn't hear your car Jack, are you down long?"

"I arrived late last night, went to the Dog House. Didn't want to upset your beauty sleep."

Over the Breaking of The Fast, and later into the morning he filled them in on his trip, the glossary, and the bits and pieces he had managed to read and maybe even understood of the writing.

They are stories Yella Man told the young Anna to record. These it appears, may be from a far bigger store of information. These mostly tell fables, like the tale of two men, who were really only one man. It seems one of them had a gift for Dream Travel. He could travel in his dreams, back in time to what he thought were better times, to enjoy them again, or to a time when he could right a wrong. He was lock keeper, on the canal, in our time, in what would be our memories, and he was alone. He knew about the Dream Travel, the American Indians believed you could use your dreams to remember incidents and people in your past. He also knew that when he was dreaming back in time he must avoid meeting his younger self. He made a mistake and both his selves crashed back to the original man's timeline, his older life. The younger self was now trapped in the future and could not return to a time where he did not exist any more.

"So do any of you remember two brothers who lived for a long time managing a Lock Passing on the canal, well upstream, from here. The somethingteenth lock?"

Heads shaking told him they did not.

"Anyway they are only stories, I think

the brothers were just figments of Yella Man's imagination. Found this in the language and in the stories. Yella Man, in describing his older self said he was 'Crubbed Up' now, I find a word for a man with a bent back is that same phrase. But maybe I'm just foostering around: fussing with this idea, that Auntie Anna wanted me to find these stories. When she was on her last gasps, she mentioned Yella Man's secret magical way. Told me to go to the wood and dream. Told me she let myself and Deirdre down. Ah well: maybe this is just some Gamsowgin, trickery, maybe even deceit, or a jocose lie. This language seems to have an expression for a lot of occasions."

THE YEW OF OLD

The Yew was old, scarified by the years of brambles and ivy and sun, night frosts and rain. It was surrounded by ferns but in the shade of the canopy these had failed to grow densely, bereft of sunlight and water, Jack thought.

It wasn't even one tree, it seemed more like several Siamese Twin trunks, each trying to escape, leaning outwards.

So this is Anna's Yew. This is where she believed the magic came from. It's maybe, a thousand years old? Older maybe. Sure, the town is only a few hundred years old, but Cultaderry the area is much older. It's a horrible stooped hulk of a tree. I thought a Yew would be taller, with a majestic trunk, but this reminds me of the body Old Yella Man had, according to Anna, small, broad and humped. Was he really a fairy: living in our world? This shambles of a majestic Yew Tree, can't be hiding any secrets!

Jack walked around the trunk, well trunks, two boles. No, it seemed to be one trunk now, and several other branches growing down, right down to the ground. Maybe even under the soil, he thought. It was an ugly bugger!

He found nothing impressive in any way. He looked higher into the twisted branches, some huge and evidently heavy. Nothing just sparse leaves and a sparkling twinkle of sky brightness. Beneath there was just the forest floor, composted where the fallen leaves had broken down. He had decided that Anna was having another laugh at all of them. Another conundrum: no magic answer.

He turned to leave; a breeze, a soft breeze on his neck made him shiver. Cold creatures, pronounced creatures that Collins lot, Anna used say, "tickled by a cold breeze on a hot day." It was not a hot day, but no wind was blowing, no breeze, just a calm.

He stood in front or the Yew tree. He had not been this deep in the wood since he had been there with Deirdre. Now he was unsure what he was doing? The message had not been clear at all, typical Anna, more conundrums.

THE YEW PRODUCED TOO SLOWLY

Some of the words in the Fingalian Glossary might have had a French language origin, so Jack was making another trip to The Lodge. If he had reasoned it out, he suspected that there were not any French words, or derivatives, but he wanted to see some of the paintings again.

Brigitte greeted him at the door, she was excited, he hoped it was to see him. "I painted another Vision Picture, that's what I feel they are. Yesterday just sitting here in the studio, I saw this. A tree with many trunks."

"Hi, nice to see you again also." Jack was scowling as he said it.

"Sorry. Hello Jack, I'm glad you returned here." She was confused, now. Happy to have another picture to show him, in her excitement she felt she may have forgotten her manners. Then she saw the wide grin on his face, and laughed as well.

"Irish humour?"

"Yes" Jack said. "Slaggin'."

The painting was of Anna's Yew, or at least it looked like it, but this one did not have as many branches growing down, neither did it have as many Siamese Twin trunks.

Brigitte explained that the picture came to her in the studio as she was sitting wondering what to paint. But as she explained it: she did not really intend to do more work, until Jack came back down. She did not say it out loud but was missing his company. She was starting to regarded him as in some way her inspiration to do more paintings in the wood. But she felt driven to sit down and produce this work, even if she had not seen The Yew on her visits to the wood.

"I never saw this in the wood." She said. "Is it there."

"It is. In a clearing, well it was a clearing, now it's getting smaller, overgrown, but the tree is there, older that this one you painted. But it's in there still.

He quoted Wordsworth.

> 'Produced too slowly ever to decay;
> Of form and aspect too magnificent
> To be destroyed.'

It was different, and the way the Yew grew this vision could have been when it was much younger, maybe even decades or maybe even a hundred years ago.

What surprise him was that this trunk was also two boles, but not as many branches trying to get back to the earth, strange that branches did not reach upward towards the light, but down towards

93

darkness. Maybe this is why people regarded the yew as sacred.

"I would paint a tree trunk as one growing, but when I tried to do that I failed. Many baby trunks..." Her telling halted, stuttered out, stooped, as if she was afraid her talent could not produce what she tried to paint.

"With all of there paintings. I don't think your creative mind was in complete control. I thought Deirdre was guiding you. But this could be an Anna intervention."

He remembered what she said before she died. "She told me to go to the wood, and dream there. She said go inside the Yew tree. I went in to visit it a while ago, the only message I got there was a cold breeze on the back of my neck."

Brigitte took a step back into the room. "I remember feeling cold as I finished this, like a ghost was walking over my grave. Learned that saying from Anna. She often shivered and said that."

"Let's have a cuppa and visit the tree. We can bring the painting and see what's changed."

On the matter of dream travel, Jack did not believe it could happen, but, over two coffees, spent some time amusing himself and Brigitte with some theories.

They wondered if two fellas in a bar were discussing the possibility and after some time one of them postulated that as it was his birthday on a certain date, and he was leaving for a new job in the States that his pal should get the bartender to put up a birthday drink for him at closing time on that day.

Then if on the next morning the drink was gone, he had travelled from some time in then future to drink it. Of course, when the time came and passed the drink was still there in the morning.

Both agreed however that if the pal in America, at some time, in the future encountered an eccentric scientist with a time machine, and the pal came back walked in and told the barman he was there for his birthday drink, it would have made headlines. They both agreed that this was something that could never happen. Until that is the first man told the story with the punchline that his pal never travelled abroad at all, and that he was just hiding out of sight, waiting to pretend he travelled back in time for his Jemmy. In Ireland in the countryside that explanation would be accepted, with the comment that the birthday boy had always been a trickster.

Both of them agreed that it would be amazing, if it really happened by time travelling, or in the case they were discussing: by Dream Travelling.

But Brigitte said. "You know the story in France, Versailles where two ladies claimed they went back in time and saw Marie Antoinette."

"They wrote a book and it was ridiculed, Mobery and Jourdain were their names.

"They wrote it under pen-names. Morison and Lamont."

Brigitte agreed this was the same tree that she encountered in her vision. It was the same but different, they both agreed as they studied the tree and the painting. "It may not be the same scene as I viewed while I painted, even if aged."

Jack assured her it was the same: a younger version of this old man before them. She shivered slightly and he felt the neck breeze as before. He moved away towards the back, kicking the ferns and stomping on the brambles catching his trouser leg. "Brambles always fight back when they think you are a danger to them. Even after you cut them and they are on the ground: when you try to pick them up they attack, always believed that."

It took a small amount of time, and some effort to traverse the symbiotic relationships of the various outgrowing branches and the downward roots. Roots were what Brigitte called the ones growing down and it seemed into the earth: it was a good description. At the back the breeze was stronger, they could hear it whistling through some obstruction or other. Maybe just closely grown branches with spaces from the wood twists: the branch shapes. Light reflected and halted by the upper sparse foliage threw strange shadows onto the bottom half of the boles, or trunks, or branches. In one spot deep into the mass of bark and moss and broken, yet not fallen, suspended broken boughs and smaller branches there was a dark, non reflective space. Jack moved closer for a better view. Abruptly he jumped back.

Brigitte screamed and asked "Is it a tree monster?"

Jack laughed and answered. "It could be, but it's more likely the monster is behind that door."

A small wooden door could be viewed inside and down a bit from his line of vision. It would be necessary to crouch down and perhaps even crawl to get inside the downward branched to get close to that portal, an entrance, if that was what it was. But a doorway to what?

They decided the answer to that, which Jack was now thinking of as an answer to Anna's Conundrum. He remembered what she said. 'Go inside the yew tree. Ask The Yew Fairy and Astarte to help.' But that journey into the Fairy Quest, should wait until they, Jack was thinking of them as together on this quest, consulted with the family.

DIRE WARNINGS

The tales, maybe even the Fairy Tales did not clear up any of the confusion Jack and the family, and now Brigitte: had about what Anna wanted them to do. The pages hidden in The Dog House although fragmented, when taken as a whole seemed to be, when loosely interpreted, to be a handbook to Astral Travel.

"But Jack explained they are hidden in the Fingalian language, and I'm not able to fully understand the gist of this: go have a dream and travel in time, backwards. What I could find out is that you can only dream, have visions of your past life."

The pages were also full of dire warnings about getting your self stuck in your dream. Something none of them understood.

"If you could get stuck in a dream of your past life," Carmel said. "I would go back and date Rock Hudson, Your mother Jack, and myself used go to his films, and eat our Emeralds out of a green package."

"You would be barking up the wrong tree there! Sister."

"But trying to turn him would be fun. I'd make him stand up, all right!"

"Back on message here, girls. What do we need

to do?"

"Jaysus Jack, read some of the stories out loud. No point in going off half-cocked." And Carmel almost choked, when she tried to swallow her tea, and laugh at the same time.

"Serves you right, if you did choke, you dirty creature." But Jeanie was now laughing as well.

When Jack had finished reading, and interpreting the pages, he asked, "Well!"

"Well me arse," Jeanie said. "You were right, just some fairy tales, that make no sense. We now know where the Auld Dear got her gift for tall tales from. Just balderdash."

Brigitte had been thinking and remembering some tales she had heard, in France and was now trying to translate the information into English.

"I have heard of people who meditate so that they can have dreams of the past and view the happenings."

Jack knew a subconscious memory had been lurking, teasing him, now he remembered. "Vision Quests, Brigitte." He said out loud. Then he tried to explain.

North American native tribes, their Shamans meditated to have and interpret dreams. They were also healers and to get a vision and maybe help heal someone they would go to a place in the wilderness to begin this journey, isolated from the outside world. They sat in a big circle and meditated, trying to calm themselves into the present. They try to stop all the static we have in our minds and trying to focus the actual vision, that is visiting them.

After the dream, the Shaman looks for evidence in a rock, feather, or some other natural relic significant to their vision.

"And it seems that they believed the experience was deeply personal, and could take an individual out of their physical body. Yella Man they said was a fairy, maybe the Native Americans and the little people are related."

A DOOR TO YELLA MANS WORLD

"It's not a real door." Eamonn Cody and Jack were standing looking down beneath the branches and briars around the Yew. "Anna had it made and placed there at some stage. Used tell us that was the way into Yella Mans World. Rubbish, but as kids we were mesmerised that a Fairy Kingdom was inside there, and if we were brave enough we could open the door and have a goo inside."

"That's it then. We can't get inside. Maybe just as well. I thought that in some way the middle was hollow. Yews can be like that, even re-root down the middle, into the earth inside and live on. That's why some called it the tree of resurrection and rebirth. Jack sounded disappointed that the mystery was not solved yet.

Eamonn paused thinking. "There is a way in. I know there is even if I never got inside, I just know if Mam said go inside the Yew, there's a way."

They walked around the tree: then walked again, left, then right, and back again. They stood close to the tree, then farther away. Looked up looked down.

"If there is a way in, it's overgrown now: gone." Jack was ready to give up and walk away, and Eamonn could not think of any reason to stop him.

"There must be a way in, Mam was a lot of things, had her secrets." Eamonn offered.

"Hid her secrets, as well." Jack added.

That bloomin breeze was back blowing on his neck, at the back of his neck. He turned to see where it might be coming from, but as he turned away from The Yew the cold on his neck turned back to a normal feeling. No breeze blew at him.

"What's up? Eamonn asked.

"Come over here and stand beside me."

Eamonn was puzzled, but moved to where Jack was pointing.

"Turn your back to the tree and move to the right. More another bit. No the other way."

Eamonn stopped moving and stood becoming more puzzled as Jack directed him to go in more small steps.

"Jaysus Jack will you make up your mind, this cold breeze is making me like one of you shivery Collins lot."

"What breeze? Move out to me a bit."

"It's gone now. Where the Feck did that come from? It's not a cold breezy day!"

Jack told Eamonn how he had felt a breeze when he visited the Yew Glade in the past. Not all over the place, just near to the downward growing branches close to where they were now standing.

"It's mad I know, but I think in some way it's coming from out of the middle of the tree."

"In Agricultural College they told us about a process where water dropping from leaves cause the temperature to fall. Maybe that's what's going on here, the dripping causing the colder air. It can happen even on a warm day. Transpir something or other." Eamonn was racking his brain for some kind of an explanation.

"Trees also cool the air by a process known as transpiration cooling. As trees release water into the atmosphere from their leaves, the surrounding air is cooled as water goes from liquid to a vapour. Remember it now."

"Could be it, that then?" Jack, however was not really accepting this as a complete solution. He felt cool breezes on his neck often.

A rustling sound caused him to turn. "I saw you move past the Lodge, I thought you might be coming here. I followed you."

"Brigitte, welcome to trying to solve the conundrum of Anna's Yew. But you know what it is. We were here before, scoping the thing out."

"Yes, but now I have decided it is different sadder, than before, and the colours are not right."

"Colours?" Eamonn asked, "How are they wrong?"

"When I first met your mother, Anna, she took me into the wood, and asked me what colours I saw in the trees. When I mentioned colours in the bark, scales of the bark. She was amused and gave me the lease on her lodge."

Eamonn was smiling. "Did she cackle?"

"She told me I used good words." Brigitte replied.

"Dems good words. Was that it?"

"Yes. Maybe she even added Begob." Brigitte said loudly, as she was moving around the tree. She bent down and stood up, looking and it seemed searching. Then she moved out of sight behind the tree. A while later she appeared moving back towards the front. She stooped and looked back into the wood, again it seemed she was searching again. Then she moved away, back into the overgrown meadow of wild flowers leading away to the side of the path they had used to approach where they were standing.

"There was another trail to the tree from out here? Was there?"

Jack looked at Eamonn. "Was there another approach?"

"Not as far as I know. Maybe there was, but not when I used come here. If there was the Old Dear never told me."

Brigitte was beckoning them towards where she was standing, urgently it seemed.

"Quick." She said. "It's changing. The light and the shadows, the twilight is changing. Look there is it much darker. Like a cave. Not twilight, what is the word? Purple light?"

"Pink?"

"No blue-green. The winkle...."

"Jees Eamonn, can you see that shadow in there?" Jack was pointing now, into the down hanging branches. Beside that thick one going into the ground. A shadow behind it seems."

"You two are colour blind, I can only see bark and leaves. Unless you mean that brown stain on the trunk. Way in there over to the right."

"That's it, but I see it as purple."

Brigitte was starting to laugh. "Anna's fairy magic colour. Like Shakespeare. He said the fairy colours were Black, Grey, Green and White. And I can see all of them in that stain. Fairy magic we all see different things, and no one of us sees the door to the cave. In French the colour would translate as taupe."

"Taupe?"

"Dark, grey, brown, like the mole."

"I'm lost here guys. What colour are we talking about?" Eamonn had a puzzled look on his face.

"It seems. All of them." Jack said. He looked towards Brigitte who nodded her head.

"Exactly. We can all see our own idea of the colour of the mole. Black, cream, grey, orange, white, even piebald. I learned this not in French but in English. My Granper had a mole story, he told in English, Irish English. As you speak it. I loved when he came to visit, lots of fairy tales as well."

Brigitte. "So are you saying you can see a door into the tree?" Jack asked.

"We will all see it when the twilight comes, when the light colours change."

"We can come back later." Eamonn said. "I'm away now for a drink. I need to get refreshments after all that. I thought for a while I was one of the bind mice in this discussion."

"Let's join him Brigitte. Now that we may have solved one of Anna's Conundrums. Into the pub, then later, hopefully into the Yew."

DARKNESS INTO LIGHT

It was only Jack who returned to try and see the entrance to the Yew. Eamonn had encountered a pal he wanted to spend more time with: and have a few more Balls O'Malt before he walked back to his own house. Brigitte had insisted he go alone to try and find Anna's secret door: insisting she would be in the way.

In the twilight he could now see the entrance, ivy overgrown with curtains of creepers disguising what he now thought was a small cave in the foliage, a tree trunk split making an entrance that maybe he could squeeze into. But first he had to negotiate a path forward through the twisted downward growing tree limbs.

The Dog House had always been a cosy hideaway. It was what Anna used call snug: comfortable, she meant, a place you could relax in. As it turned out on this day when Jack visited it was also a place where you could fall asleep easily: and dream.

A young girl was skipping along a woodland pathway, but her steps were silent, making no sound, even though she was on a trail full of leaves and fallen nuts, hazel and chestnut. The image was being viewed from behind as if the dreamer was following the girl. She turned often, smiling and silently laughing, beckoning calling to the follower. Or maybe even followers: more than one?

Occasionally she pointed a way forward. That way, that way, she seemed to be saying. Follow me a while longer. Suddenly, as all dreams do, a new picture emerged. Now they were in a wooden hut. It had a wooden inside roof, but the beams were irregular, bumpy, and in places the planks were shining, burnished, well worn, but again at the edges the dream vision room was dark. It was a dark the follower feared. A place he did not want to go towards.

The girl was smiling as she sat on a wooden bench at the back wall of the hut. And then the scene changed again as they – and now the dreamer knew they were together, the girl and the follower.

It appeared they were now it seemed, in a Picture House, that phrase rather than a cinema suggested itself into his mind. The sepia scene was showing a woman wrapping a newborn baby in a blanket, swaddling cloths, the phrase came into the mind of the dreamer.

The scene faded and Jack started to wake up. "We will call him after you, John," the woman said.

The man replied, "Fair enough, but can we make it Jack."

Jack was awake now, remembering the dream, and gasping for breath: for air. Anytime he pulled a turtle neck jumper over his head, or as a lad struggled to pull a tight jumper back over his head, he felt the same feeling.

"I always thought that feeling was a throw back to my birth. 'Forty eight hours it took me to squeeze you out. You brat. Remember all that pain? No! Well I do!'"

Jack remembered the loose pages, he now regarded as Yella Man's fables. His stories, with the codicil, remember you can only have dream visions of your own life time, your own experiences. And now his journey along that path would start with a vision of his birth.

Anna, he thought, not for the first time: what one of your adventures do you want me to follow? That girl, the dancing, prancing, skipping guide to the hut he now believed was a young Anna. But where the heck was that hut?

FADED PAGES
IN TIME

Yella Man's journal, was dictated to the young Anna. Finally, Jack was getting somewhere with reading it, translating the words and sentences from Fingalian and Midland Gaelic, into some kind of tales, fables more like. They were filled with more warnings than encouragement to believe they would help, in some way. Anna had spoken on 'Yella Man's Magical Secret Way', but if it was in here he could not see it.

As far as Jack could understand it: there was no magic in the tales, no secret way to do anything. He was sure Anna had meant heal the pain, but who did this pain belong to?

Eamonn had an idea and he came to Jack in the Dog House to discuss it. "Strim a path to the entrance – with a brush cutter. After all you own the wood and it's about time you did some real work."

So they scoped out the yew and selected what they thought would be the entrance and strimmed their way in, and around, and behind the branches or roots that grew, out from and around the trunk.

Finally they had a narrow winding unkept lawn pathway, through the brambles that now gave access to what they thought was a cave style entrance in the trunk.

"It's very narrow." Jack ventured, "But maybe someone could squeeze inside. Don't know about getting back out though."

"Well." Eamonn ventured. "Away with you. If you are not back by teatime I will send the girls in to pull you out. But maybe if you are away with the fairies you might stay there. Don't vanish on me now!"

Jack cork-popped himself in through the entrance. The inside, resembled the panelled room of his dream. It was a cave indeed, a cave inside the empty bole of the yew. A stalactite of twisted grey green, root matter dropped from the ceiling into the ground. So this is the resurrection root of a dead yew, he thought. A small bench of more twisted sideways lying ground roots seemed to invite him to sit. The interior was lighted from above, in some way the sun was sending viable light beams of water droplets and colours in rainbows shapes onto the clay floor. Strangely devoid of weeds or grass tuft growth. Jack was feeling serene. Just like he did as a boy visiting a church for a quick prayer when passing. The memory almost made him cross himself in the usual blessing: Father, Son and Holy Spirit.

He was back at the farmhouse, just in time for "Tae and Sweet Cake" the usual Sunday afternoon snack.

And some conversation. All he had to tell was that he found a way into the Yew but that was about the gist of it as Eamonn put it.

"No advance then. In the search for a happy ending. What?" he added looking at the horrified faces of the group. "The auld dear sent him off on a wild goose chase, that's the gist of it. Another conundrum. Not a happy dream at all, a nightmare."

"I didn't fall asleep in there! Could that be it? Give me more tae. Has anyone got the spell book? Maybe I can spell myself to sleep."

"Bullshit Jack." Carmel responded. "It's a cure book. Not a potion's book. Well it is but not ones that will send you off to Noddy Land."

She retrieved the book from a table drawer. "Threw it in there when you gadded off to Dublin to meet your other fancy woman Jack."

"Right. Now can anyone remember where, between what pages, the loose pages were? I wonder can where they were be significant? I can't think of any other way to try and solve the conundrum. It's a long shot."

There was no way at this stage any of them could remember or re-assemble where the loose pages had been. Jack was starting to consider that the two, the loose pages and the Cure or Spell Journal held some significant clue in their placement. As of now he could not understand the sequence or link or what ever it was.

Eamonn was fingering through the pages. "Maybe if we select a few, maybe take a word or two and see how we might link them if we needed to. Anna, Mam that is, would not have made it so hard we couldn't find an answer. After all she spent a lot of time berating me for not using my big brain as she called it. Come at it another way, as both herself and your dad, would advise Jack."

Tess held up a page. "This one is about dreaming your problems away. And I'm sure the other book had a potion for sweet dreams as well. In fact Mam used send me with a bottle to Auntie Seaver told me to tell her to get a good sleep with sweet dreams. Well you lot get searching."

As it turned out there was only one real spell, as they were now calling the so called cures, for a sleep potion. Others were similar but not as specific as the one with the title 'Soothing Dreams For Troubled Minds' .

"I'm trying to remember who Auntie Seaver was? Was she Lady Gaa Gaa? The woman who was always away with the fairies? She drooped spits on me often enough, when she hugged me. Smelled awful as well. Not our aunt though, someone else's."

The recipe was for some herbs they knew by sight, some would need some research though.

"Cross of Christ! Don't any of yees shake yer bustles, 'til I'm back." Janie was away out the door like her backside was on fire.

"Bet she knows where to find the ingredients."

A while later Janie returned with a small basket containing bottles, powered ingredients in small cans, that once held polish, and some glass demijohns. Miniature demijohns with lug handles that only a small finger would fit into.

"Forgot this Jack. It's a present for you from Mam. Gave it to me a few months ago. To hold for you. That fella will need this she said. Keep it 'till he needs it."

"More tae, anyone? Let's have a look at this new conundrum."

Some of the bottles had brown labels tied to the necks. They were not as faded as they expected, of fact one or two seemed new. Or maybe these bottles had been prepared a while ago, not as they would have thought long ago.

Some of the newer labels had Annas Copperplate writing. At first glance they noted it seemed to be gibberish, definitely not English, or any other language they recognised.

"Wonder is this French" Carmel wondered, then she answered her own question. "No, it's not froggie croaks."

Jack tried reading one. " Ahaygar Buddlehin Causey Crit Crub Dawk Dhrig Slug (No, No.) Scraith

Scaird ShanAthar.

They agreed it seemed to be gibberish, and the other labels and notes, some in English some in this strange language, almost a chanting language, was just as confusing.

Jack cleared off for a while to ring Connie the Fingalian expert.

"Well this is what Connie thinks it is. But she is confused as the words don't seem to be a label, or a sentence. More of a warning or directions as to how the liquid in the bottle should be used. Starting with this word Ahaygar, in Fingalian that word is used in a sensitive case, like beloved one." He went on to try and explain that the other words were also confusing.

"Buddledin is sipping, like ducks, or dabbing hands in water. She thought Causey was path. Crit was what they called a hunchback, or maybe a person who was cold. On the hunchback idea Crub would be to stoop down, maybe to enter a low door. Dawk would be to be pricked with a thorn. Dhrig, the Dregs of a bottle, as we say the last drop. To Slug would be take a big swig, a gulp out of a bottle. No slugs, or gulps then, just sips. A Scraith is a passage. In Cavan they still call a boreen a street. Scaird I think is a syringe. And the last two she hasn't a clue but maybe they are a signature. Old father or it could be a person who is small, or who stopped growing."

Carmel has been writing down the words and

the possible meaning. Now she tried to provide a sensible translation.

"Beloved. Sip a path. Hunchback, stoop down. What else could he do? This is rubbish. What comes next?"

She consulted her list. "Prick yourself, with the dregs of a bottle. No, now it says take a Slug from the bottle. A passage and a syringe. All this from a dwarf. Or a small ...Person maybe a fairy message. That's the only bit to make sense. The Auld Dear was away with the fairies when she wrote this."

Jack added. "Maybe the words should not be read as a sentence, or in order. There must be a message here. I would want to know if it's directions or a warning, before I sipped any of this. Maybe you don't sip it, you rub it on somewhere."

"Or other. Ha ha.."

"Could it be a warning of what not to do?"

"So maybe sip some of this then go down the path stooping down like a hunchback. Go in the low door. Then I'm lost, unless like a lot of instructions or some priests preaching, the ones who are also teacher, or professors in colleges, the instructions are repeated to make sure the message sinks in.

'So maybe sip don't slug the liquid. Dawk we though was was a thorn scratch, but I remember Anna calling one of the old neighbours A Daw, A Gob Daw, a foolish fellow, she said."

"She loved that word all right."

"And maybe don't drink the last dregs of the

liquid. The passage might mean the path to the past. We will never know unless I try it, sometime. Yea sometime? Not today. We need more research."

THE VISIT AND RECONCILIATION

He was in The Yew Bole, all the time for talking and wondering, and supposing was over, Jack thought.

He remembered the advice Kyrl always gave his students Be Brave. That advice and taking small risks helped him in life. Now he sat with the bottle labelled Sweet Dreams For Troubled Minds, it will do the trick he thought or drive me Gaa Gaa like Auntie Seaver, Lady Gaa Gaa, as she was always away with the fairies. He had picked the time carefully, and made sure the family, his midland minders were unsure he had decided to, maybe take his life in his hands and sip from the spell bottle.

It was not the original small Demi John contents, but a new concoction that they had all researched and collected the ingredients as per what they thought were Anna's recipe and directions.

Carmel shook the bottle vigorously when it was needed, and twirled her body around whispering incantations, she said. But all she was doing was reciting and old poem Anna had taught her. Similar she said to the one in Macbeth, eye of newt and the like. Double double toil and trouble. Fire burn and cauldron bubble.

He approached the strimmed path to the entrance to the Yew Bole remembering what they thought had been the instructions. *So maybe sip some of this,* he took a sip from his Demi John, then go down the path *stooping down like a hunchback.* He bent forward, and slipped in between the twisted down swept branches. He want inside and sat on another form like seat. He took another sip from the bottle and waited for sleep.

It was a vivid dream. A waking dream within a real dream. Jack had had ones like this before. Ones where he was a newspaper editor, editing or composing a story. It was dreams like this that started him thinking he could be a writer. The news stories were well constructed and well researched and were full of detail. A good researcher reporter tale. This happening was the same. In his wakey up dream, he was in the Yew, on the bench, looking up and out at the stars in some way visible. How he got here, or travelled here he did not know. One minute it seems he was in Dublin preparing to attend a function. Now here in Port, some bits of clothing, old and torn, worn out by time, around him and under his feet, The trousers around his ankles. He wanted to go outside, leave the dream room, but he was almost naked. In his dream he laughed – Anna you did not mention that if I had a time travel dream my clothes would not survive the trip. he thought of some information he had found. A person could dream travel back in the years of their life. Never forward. But things could change, and it's important to try and not deliberately change   anything. Otherwise your world, as you know it, could come crashing down on you and you could get stuck like the Lock Keepers. *I thought that was one of her tall tales.*

So there it is. This is where this dream will end. Nevertheless before he awoke he was going to take a peep outside. Maybe the wood is gone and he is in the wilderness or in a fairy fort.

But the wood was there outside looking pretty much the same. However, leaning up alongside a tree was what he could swear was his bike from years ago. He often wanted to travel around the country on that bike, break out from only local trips, then he remembered Bobby, born with a heart condition. They said Bobby has a weak heart. But he started cycling and often went out of Laoghis across Offaly and into Connaught and returned in the one day. Seán Kelly before Seán Kelly.

Just A Mo! His bike did not have a bag, or a messenger boy's basket, a wicker woven hamper, on the handle bars, or on the rere carrier- a travel bag! Quickly, he ran out and retrieved it back into the Yew Cave. The bag had what looked like his Corduroy Jacket, the one he thought suited his athletic build of his youth: broad shoulders from the weight training and thick neck muscles: that aided his fast sprint starts, propelling him away at the starting shot. Wrapped inside were shoes, and a shirt, a jocks wide and baggy, someone else's: he thought. And a trousers: nondescript but, the real deal he realised, for a time when he should have been home, visiting Deirdre.

These looked like the clothes he left behind when he moved to Dublin and discovered that suits were the uniform of a Civil Servant.

Suited and booted, slip on boots with high insteps, almost western style. He was now prepared to move out and go down into the town. He shook his shoulders, squared his frame and put his hand into his right trouser pocket. Anna always said, search for a hankie: our tribe are snotters. Inside indeed was a hankie: and a note, Anna's Copperplate: a warning.

'On the nights when the little girl is seriously ill, for a while, before she goes. I will leave your bike here, and collect it again in the morning, if needs be. If you are reading this you better know you are on a serious journey with disastrous consequences if you change the past terribly. I'm hoping that you have discovered the Yew Bole and the magic it can weave in your dreams.

Be safe Jack, I hope both of you get peace. Be so, so, careful. Anna.'

Anna had hoped he would find the clues, solve the conundrum and dream travel back to this night, and go and visit Deirdre: put things right. He must hurry, before this dream ends and leaves him miserable for all time, if he messed up what he thought was an opportunity to heal his torment. He knew now that despite the fact he hid his anguish, it was there gnawing at him: eating him inside, eventually it would conquer him with perhaps terrible consequences.

But first, before the visit he had a task to complete. One he had thought about and planed for years, but never achieved: his gift from their love-nights asking forgiveness.

So that night in the moonlight under the stars, he took the wicker woven hamper and went out into the wood, heading for its pine heart. There he garnered from the forest floor into the hamper, the mulch of small twigs and pine and fir and larch cones, and covered them with palm; then moving outward seeking, took the brown and yellow and green turning to amber fallen-sinner-leaves and covered them with creeping ivy; then the hawthorn haws, yew berries and the green spiky chestnuts, vulva-open, showing their fruits inside.

He went and stole from gardens jasmine, lavender and bramble and from bogs he took heather and their peat. Then at morning early, but also late, he took his treasure trove of forest, bog and garden to the house, her father's door, where he stood in his day-clothes.

He carried the captured autumn night-time to her. In that bittersweet bower, he surrounded her with woodland. Giving her soft air born of pine fronds that wafted chestnut smells and whirling seeds of sycamore, and made for her the rustling sounds of leaves wind-tossed against the fallen bark of ash and beech. As sacred as any priest of pipe and plug, he prepared between his palms a tobacco of peat and heather, and dropped the chaff along the floor and blew the fragrance to the air. He scattered the gardens on her bed.

He told her he was sorry and called her his first love. She smiled and reached up her small hand. He took her hand and kissed her cheek. As the day filled their new wood with light they murmured of the old days and never spoke about the present

The family left them alone that day and they whisper-talked, remembering. She dozed and then they whispered again and then she dozed again. Together they waited.

In that Blackthorn Month, at that Sacred Night of The Yew: the night of death and rebirth, transformation and reincarnation; Deirdre died.

Then they wrapped her and hid her away: carrying her, the heart of the coffin-wood, that once hid pine martins, squirrels, owls and sleepy, hot-foot-hopping, pigeons.

IN THE NEW TIME

In that time of the starting of the new story, the following morning, Auntie Anna went to the wood and found the bike was still there. It was not where she had parked it and when she looked around she found the bag, lying empty inside in the yew bole, and the Wicker Basket was missing.

She smiled first, then howled a wild terrible shriek of glee, and joy, not pain. Shouted, over and over again. "Good man Jack. You did it. You Scamp. You fixed it. Well done Jack. I knew you would figure it all out. Bedad you did, so you did. Well done. Well done, Bedad."

Then she went back towards home constantly checking if the wood as she had know it was still looking the same. It was. But to her, the light in the trees was brighter, and the birdsong was sweeter, and the path as she walked down the small hill had ruts from bicycle wheels, and the dew was glistening on the grass.

To Anna this was a new morning and she was at peace with the tranquil solace, the healing she thought she detected in her wood.

When Jack awoke he was bursting for a pee. The

discomfort was so bad he decided to stand and do the job inside. He did not think the pain would allow him walk outside. First time ever he thought I will be pissing on a tree: from inside. He reached down to open his zip, only he did not have a zip on the trousers he was wearing. Buttons? A button up fly? Old fashioned and not what I was wearing when I came in here. This get-up is not mine! He was recalling parts of the dream. In that I woke up naked and found these clothes. In a basket on my old bike, then....it was hazy he could only remember riding somewhere on the bike. His calf muscles certainly thought he had been exercising: something he had not done is a long time. His arms were sore as well. Was I riding a bike fast and pulling on the handle bars to climb up a hill, or something like that. And this old suit. Where did that come from and did some of the girls or Eamonn dress me up in this when I was sound asleep? Then he remembered that it was like his corduroy coat: his old blazer and the pants that she wore to match his sartorial elegance. And the slip on boots with the elasticated side, and the slight heels. Real Cool Man!

I need to get out of here and talk to Anna's crowd.

The wood was the same, he was sure of that: yet, he was feeling a dread, and he had no idea why that should be. He felt the same, as far as he knew he looked the same. So all must be right with life. Life? Yes he felt more alive, more serene. The dream was vivid, but it was only a dream, so that could not have lightened his mood, his grasp on life. Dream Time

Travel My Arse. He could almost hear Anna's voice in his head. He saw the lodge in the trees. He decided to visit Brigitte and tell her what had happened, or what he thought had happened.

He approached the front door, and he had no idea why. Normally it would have been that he would go around the back: to the door there. Never really since the first day had he approached the front entrance. It was closed and he knocked with his palm on the wood. He banged louder, harder and the door moved a little. It was obviously not locked only latched shut, so he opened the old fashioned lever with his thumb and he could hear the hasp rise and the door started to open. A mad barking greeted his attempt to move in, loud and harsh? No. Strangely not strident, more he thought a nice to see you greeting.

The coal black, shiny coated Cocker Spaniel was dancing around in front of him. Seemingly delighted to see him. Jack reached down and patted his head. "Nice to see you also boy. But who are you and where did you come from? Are you a stray or is Brigitte minding you for someone?" He had not met this animal before. So it was a complete mystery as to why the dog was greeting him like a long lost friend.

Always said dogs could read a mind, or sense feelings, this lad knows I'm relaxed and no danger to him.

Jack started to move into the entrance hall, and immediately sensed something had changed. It took a few seconds to realise that the painting that he had seen on the wall of the the one he called The Dancing Embrace was missing. Strange that. I wonder why Brigitte moved it. The sitting room was different as well, not that of a single woman, more a family room with some toys and other things young children would play with.

Careful Jack backed out of the house. Something's wrong here he thought.

He want around to the back door. When he opened it the dog was waiting silent and he could swear smiling at him. AGAIN!

The kitchen was tidy the furniture lived in but clean. Then he noticed a note pinned among the other scraps on a notice board. It caught his eye, because it had his name on the folded page. JACK.

The note was plain, but confusing. Can you collect the girls from school. I need to get some groceries. *She always called them groceries: he said the messages.* And feed Alfie, if it's around lunch time when you return. There's a message for you, from Cowboy and Aoife. They want all of us to go down to Kilkenny. To the Ranch for her birthday.

Even though he was in complete shock, *Aoife and Cowboy?* by instinct he opened a cupboard reached in retrieved a plastic container of dog food, and a dish and poured out some for Alfie.

I'm still dream travelling he thought. None of this is real. Aoife, we were married and she died. So....

As far as he could work out something had gone terribly wrong. he recalled waking inside in the yew. But now it could be that his body was still in there in a dream and this was not reality, just a continuing dream. Turning into a nightmare now. He could almost hear his father's voice in his head advising: start again at the start and work the puzzle out. *Where to start though? The Graveyard her grave.*

He stood for a while at the Iron Gate. *At least I remember the colour. Grey like the railings.*

Looking toward the grave: Deirdre's grave he noticed a couple standing there in prayer. Yes he remembered, people down here visit the graveyard and tour the graves, particularly ones that may not have many visitors.

Slowly he moved in closer. Content to wait until the couple were moving on. He could see the gravestone and part of the inscription. 'Here lies Deirdre Rachel...'

Then he noticed the bottom left corner of the upright slab had a carving of a bike basket. He knew it would depict overflowing greenery, small twigs and pine and fir and larch cones, and brown and yellow and green turning to amber fallen-sinner-leaves covered with creeping ivy, hawthorn haws, yew berries and the green spiky chestnuts, vulva-open, showing their fruits inside.

The man noticed him when he turned briefly to check who the intruder was. He turned back and put his arm around the woman. " It's just the Collins boy." He said softly.

"Glad to see you Jack." She said. "Visiting Deirdre again. Aren't you. Nice to see you. How are the family?"

But it can't be. Both of you died of broken hearts after she died. I saw this stone with your names on it.

He remembered his feelings clearly. *She wasn't*

alone any more: her parents, were buried beside her. That in itself caused a pang of sadness, a slight tightening in the chest, a queasy feeling down low in the stomach: a memory of a time when he thought that in the end, they would lie side by side. It wasn't anything they talked about, or even planned, but down there in that country town husbands and wives usually ended up that way: twin plots one headstone; beloved wife devoted husband.

His mind was whirling. But that was then: and now is now. Either I'm still dreaming. Or things changed and Anna warned about changing things. Will I be like the Lock Keepers? All for one and one for all. He laughed at the idea. Inside however he was terrified.

"Fine. Mrs. Eames." He replied again by instinct.

What family? I don't have a family. "Have I one?" He muttered out loud.

"Now Jack joking again. You scamp. Of course you have. Those girls? Dotes pure dotes always had great manners. Calls us Missus and Mister. Must be the mother's influence, Hazel. Definitely not this fella."

Jack said bye and moved away. *That note was for me. I'm not still dreaming am I? Anna's house. Have to go there.*

Carmel heard his steps on the gravel and came out of the house. She took one look at him and started laughing.

"Jees! Jack were you at a fancy dress? Sixties style? Hey girls put on the kettle, and we will have another laugh at this fella. I hope your little girls haven't seen you in that get up. Hold on a sec. Did you find them in the Dog House? I thought the Auld Dear stored some of your duds in there, a long time ago. Must be dusty and smelly if that's where you got them, for the party?

But then Jack." she said. "What's time to any of us? Just A fleeting dream? I knew from the cut of Mam that she would fix things somehow. Maybe she was not the only witch or wizard in the family."

"Carmel is this real? Am I back?"

"Since I don't know what you are talking about I am tempted to ask from where? But I feel Jack you need to know: you are back. Even though I don't know what you are talking about. But you have that traveller look about you. Mam always told me to watch you for it. Now I think I see it in your eyes. Which by the way, used to be blue, now they're brown. Now you really are as Buddy sang: A Brown Eyed Handsome Man."

And she walked back into the house singing her own made up lyrics to the song.

"Flying across the bogs in a bagger machine... Diddy Diddy ...I saw a Brown Eyed Handsome Man...Diddy Diddy...."

Reader:

I hope you enjoyed this small book. It took me a very long time to write it. It was to be my first book. Unfortunately it may well be my last!

Old Father Time beckons, and I don't know where my lifetime hours and days have slipped away to.

Slán,

Lazarian Wordsmith.

June 21st. 2023

... sometime around the year 560, Saint Columba became involved in a quarrel with Saint Finnian, over a psalter.

Columba copied the manuscript and intending to keep the copy. Saint Finnian disputed his right to keep the copy.

Thus, this dispute was about the ownership of the copy.

King Diarmait mac Cerbaill gave the judgement, to Finian, "To every cow belongs her calf, therefore to every book belongs its copy."

ABOUT THE AUTHOR

Lazarian Wordsmith

In Ireland of the distant past, names denoted trades. John Carpenter, David (the) Smith, Jack Miller, Billy Farmer. These are translations of the original Irish names. When I decided to use a pen name I followed the tradition. Since my third name is Lazarian and I wanted to write well, I aspired to be Lazarian Wordsmith.

Lazarian Wordsmith is an evolving human being: trying to live life to its full potential - among the Fingal Hills- in Ireland. In another existence he has been an actor, broadcaster, script writer, historian, environmental campaigner, a radio producer and he also worked in the Airline Industry.His friends deny this - saying he was employed there. He tries to craft stories on the anvil of his imagination.

Sometimes he even succeeds....

BOOKS BY THIS AUTHOR

In The Wicker Wood Where Secrets Are Buried

The time is Ireland in a fragile peace deal, after the Northern Ireland Ceasefire. George Edward Bowen believes he is dying from terminal cancer. He has sin on his soul and although not a Catholic he wants Priestly Absolution for the girls he kidnapped and killed. He abducts Father Jim Gaffney.

Bishop Sylvester Mahon, who is also hiding secrets, contacts his old IRA acquaintance Shane O'Neill and asks him to find and rescue Gaffney.

When Sonny Mc Entaggart finally finds out who his father is – he is on the run from the authorities.

He is using the alias, Shane O'Neill.

The Knowledge Seekers & The Land Of

Cudhabeen

These are short stories and poems from the writer's imagination yet influenced by the tales and poems of the Irish Céilí house gatherings.

Peggy's Secret, Streets Of Birdsong, Buteo Buteo

Stories from Midland Ireland based on memories of the 1960's. The people, places and happenings that helped mould a teenager.